DORSET COUNTY LIBRARY

204219913 V

Badlands in My Blood

Rated as the finest trail scout in north-west Texas, Steve Walker would guide anybody to any place they wanted to go in the vast wilderness of the badlands. Except one. He never spoke of the party he'd taken into the forbidding Twisted Hills region, said by some to contain a haunted and secret place called Quivira – City of Gold. All they knew was that job had cost him his girl, his reputation and his peace of mind – but not his courage.

Then came Rogan with an offer he could not refuse, and so the scout agreed to escort the rich man's party to Quivira – for a price. But it wasn't enough and Steve Walker realized this too late.

Now he had nothing but his guns and grit to pit against the outlaw hellions of the badlands and the ghosts of the past.

By the same author

Shannon
Five Guns From Diablo

Badlands in My Blood

Dempsey Clay

© Dempsey Clay 2004
First published in Great Britain 2004

ISBN 0 7090 7568 5

Robert Hale Limited
Clerkenwell House
Clerkenwell Green
London EC1R 0HT

The right of Dempsey Clay to be identified as
author of this work has been asserted by him
in accordance with the Copyright, Designs and
Patents Act 1988.

Typeset by
Derek Doyle & Associates, Liverpool.
Printed and bound in Great Britain by
Antony Rowe Limited, Wiltshire

CHAPTER 1

THE GODLESS BREED

Walker drifted.

It was mostly what he did these days, this tall, gaunt-faced man of the badlands seated astride the heavy-chested Cheyenne gelding, which along with his Winchester and a pair of Colt .45s seemed about all he had left of value in the aftermath of the the last guide job he'd bossed – the one that went to hell and gone wrong.

But the harsh country still drew him as it had always done, and he knew it was still infinitely better than the town, his lonely room or the saloon, despite the stinging flurries of sand that whipped capriciously up from nowhere, forcing him to duck his head and hold on to his hat until it passed, each rough gust leaving the land panting and heat-stricken in its wake.

He pushed on, a single speck of life under a sun pouring relentless heat upon the earth. Kept drifting vaguely north-east into the nothingness, each mile carrying him further from civilization, if Sulphurville on Clay Creek could ever rate as civilized. Rippling in the shimmering heat, the clusters of rocks surrounding him seemed to float and move like bloated corpses in a yellow flood. And when he lifted his gaze the mirages pulsated and tantalized until they formed the images of human shapes and faces which he recognized, savage faces framed in golden helmets, screaming their silent hatred at him from the sky ... the terrified, pleading face of the woman he would never see again.

Time for a jolt.

He unscrewed the cap of the canteen, tipped it to his lips and opened his throat. Half water and half rye seemed just about the perfect blend for this man of the trails these days: these post-Twisted Hills days as distinct from better times when he'd never touch a drop from the time he set out with a party from base until his return.

But everything was different now. He was no longer Walker, top trail scout in north-west Texas, the man with an unblemished record. The expedition to Gun City had laid him low, and now he felt like just any other drifter who drank too much at Garvin's saloon and morosely chose to keep most of the details of his one and only botched job to himself.

About all the badlands knew of his last journey was that he'd lost a man and a woman and that Comancheros had been inolved. Such violent episodes were all too common in this vast and primitive corner of the south-west, and the only one to point an accusing finger at Walker had been Walker himself. But that was enough. More than enough to keep the liquor flowing and the big gelding slogging on through heat, dust and distance until the man from Sulphurville would either snap out of it or run out of luck, always a big chance for any man who dared risk riding this land alone.

The country flattened and widened here, was tinged rust-red. Brutally beautiful, it was like the end of the earth and no place for mankind. Yet man continually intruded here, whether prompted by greed, necessity, bravado, desperation or venality. They came and they went, and sometimes they paid Steve Walker big money to guide them across the dangerous miles, for it was claimed he knew the Kree Badlands better than any white man alive, a reputation of which he had been justly proud until the incident in the shadow of Spanish Mountain brushed it all away, just as the rising wind was now sweeping up the powder-dry reaches of Condor Valley in great rolling billows of red dust around him today.

And in his sight the dust seemed to mould itself into the cloud of auburn hair streaming back from Cora Lee's stricken white face in that last horrifying moment before the warrior's golden lance struck her and drove her over the sheer drop to her death. . . .

Walker blinked the image away and was sleeving his lips and staring off at nothing when something in that immensity of distance, some faint, almost imperceptible flicker of movement caught the corner of his eye.

Reining in on a low bluff, reaching for his binoculars, he stared directly north-west against the slant of the sliding sun, at what? A speck of life. No. More than one. Two ... three tiny dots of black moving against the backdrop of a gaunt yellow cliff which marked the mouth of just one of several wide canyons gapping the valley walls out there.

As he sharpened the focus his muscles suddenly locked with shock. Ashen, raging and impotent, he watched cold-blooded murder being done before his very eyes.

The distance was great but the binoculars were powerful. There was a running man afoot and two figures behind on horseback, raising their sixguns. The frantic lopsided gait of the runner suggested to the watcher just who this runty figure in shabby wasteland garb might be, but that brace of piebald mules, watching dumbly from the sidelines, put it beyond any doubt. Gimpy Flint it was without question, and this hardy little hermit, desert rat and survivor of the badlands for several years to Walker's knowledge, had plainly suddenly run out of luck, without a generous share of which no loner could hope to make old bones in this country.

The grey-rigged gunmen on tall black horses were a stink in the nostrils, a stye in the eye and foul anathema to every badlander in general and to Steve Walker in particular.

Comancheros. The Enemy People. Last encountered by this trail scout in the Twisted Hills south of Spanish Mountain the awful day his woman died. These scavengers of the outlands were so often the last human beings ever sighted by those reckless people who ventured here and never returned. The Comancheros had drawn blood on that worst day of his life, were about to do so again without his being able to do a blessed thing to prevent it.

The killers were allowing the runt to run, one leg lunging, the other dragging in the dust. Most likely the killers had 'promised' to spare his miserable life if he should prove able to run out of range before they got their long-handled revolvers working, he thought. That would be a Comanchero's notion of fun.

Although the gimp was less than a thumbnail high in Walker's augmented vision, he imagined he could see desperate hope warring with the certainty of imminent death working the rat's weathered features as that one good leg and a bummer continued to pump frantically beneath him, his arms flailing like windmills, the hat bouncing by its chinstrap against skinny shoulders.

He saw the tiny puffs of gunsmoke erupt against the blackness of the horses and the grey of their riders long moments before the muffled reports reached him across the singing distance. By then Gimpy Flint was a tiny ball rolling through thick dust that rose around him like water, rolling slower and slower now, despite the cruel lead that continued to hammer into him. Until this little kit fox of the desert was still and the grey wolves astride the dark horses were riding slowly away.

Walker shuddered.

The Comancheros' horses were carrying them towards the welcoming maw of Falcon Canyon. Naturally they were making westward now. Their lair which none knew of lay somewhere out there beyond the setting sun; he at least knew that much. From out of the west they came and went like grey ghosts of the Panhandle, just as they had been doing through long and bloody decades of Texas history and might well continue to do long after Walker's time was done.

But almost unconsciously as he sat his saddle there letting the fierce heat soak into his bones, the scout was aware of his memory-map unfolding. It showed his mind's eye the five canyons spreading away from Condor Valley out there like the fingers of a spread hand; the closest, the 'thumb' canyon that angled sharply south-west, being Falcon.

No, Falcon Canyon wasn't the Comanchero headquarters. None of the five canyons was. But Falcon was a known campground and sometime staging-post for the grey raiders, the kind of familiar place they might head for after satisfying themselves with yet another kill. . . .

He felt his neck hair lift and his left hand fell to the canteen. He had no way of knowing whether what he was thinking might simply be the result of rye whiskey hitting an empty gut, or if it was just the natural reaction from a man with more anger inside him than he could rightly contain just now.

He stared east. Fifty miles of familiar trail with the security of Sulphurville at the end of it.

He turned back to the west. Maybe he had one chance in a hundred of running down those killers. Providing they stuck to the Falcon trail, or didn't get to link up with more of their own slinking pot-hound kind *en route*, that was. Some choice! Yet even the suspicion that he might well be making a reckless decision here didn't hold him back for more than a few seconds before he suddenly jerked the horse's head around towards the three o'clock sun and used his heels.

What he had in mind wouldn't do Gimpy Flint one lick of good now, he well knew. Any more than it would help the people who'd died out in the Twisted Hills. But just maybe it would help Steve Walker – if it didn't kill him first.

It was almost evening. Chuckwallers and lizards scuttled out of Walker's way, raising little puffs of dust in their wake. The gelding was too weary to shy. It moved along ploddingly, head hanging, neck sheened with sweat. By contrast the rider rode ramrod erect and fully alert as he put the canyon behind him to move on into tumbling broken country, streaked and crosshatched by flung shadows and dry watercourses.

The killers' trail could be read with ease. He saw where they had loped, where they had halted, paused to feed their horses or swerved to avoid a snake. Plainly they were not expecting pursuit. They'd killed, robbed, and were now unhurriedly heading for the remote wastes that they ruled. He could envisage them as they travelled, lean, saddle-hardened figures with cruel and alien faces, saddle-bags most likely stuffed with plunder, travelling westward in leisurely fashion and likely anticipating a hero's homecoming at whatever foul hole in the dirt they might call home, when and if they got there.

If.

Taut muscles worked visibly beneath the bronze of his jawline as Walker pushed on. Recklessness, if that was what was driving him now, was rarely part of his nature. But neither was losing people who'd entrusted their lives to his care. Everything had changed for him in recent times, including the rules. He was a very different man from his pre-Twisted Hills days, and it was hatred, bitterness and rye whiskey that spurred him on in pursuit of the grey scum who had killed just once too cruelly today. He'd managed to convince himself that if Stephen Hawkwind Walker didn't balance out the scales for this crime then his failure might somehow compound what had happened the last time he'd ventured this far from civilization.

He scowled.

Maybe he should ease up on the hooch?

There were thickets here where the rough ground began to rise towards broken ridges. He lost the faint trail several times but hunted round until he picked it up again. It wasn't too long before the name Hill Spring filtered into his mind. He figured he was within maybe five miles of the only high water available in all this desolate country's thousands of square miles. Comancheros might be capable of existing without morals, conscience or even a shred of humanity, but even they must have water just like any other predators of the wild country.

A half-hour later he reined in at the base of a shaggy hill. Small brown birds were pecking at the fresh horse-droppings scattered beneath clumps of manzanita as he dragged a vesta into life along his thigh and set a cigarette alight. His narrowed eyes were on the hilltop. If memory served him right, and it almost always did out here, Hill Spring should be the first feature he saw when he topped out this rise.

He swung down and shook his muscles loose in the shade cast by a live oak. Christ, it was still murderously hot.

He soaked his bandanna from the canteen and wiped the gelding's tongue. The critter was growing used to whiskey-flavoured water these days. He poured a little into his hat and as the animal slurped it up, Walker drew his Colts and checked them out.

No longer questioning his decision to track the killers, he was filled with ice-cold determination as he watched the setting sun move the shadows across the slopes. Light was beginning to drain from the air. He swung up and settled into the leather, the gelding grunting beneath his weight. He rode straight to the crest of the slope where he sighted two things dead-ahead. The little brown hill topped out by a cluster of sycamores which shielded the spring was the first, the second being the hindquarters of a horse protruding from the trees a short distance away to the left.

Pay-dirt, he told himself.

Only thing, there plainly wasn't enough cover on the raddled and shade-strewn slopes of that brown hill to hide a fully grown gnat, much less a tall man on horseback.

The old Walker would surely have taken cover, calmly to figure out his battle plan at this point. But this vengeance-driven Walker was too primed to back up so much as an inch, and instead slid silently to the earth.

He drew the Winchester from the scabbard which went limp as the blued barrel cleared it. It was true, so he reminded himself grimly, that the Comancheros had not been the prime villains in the north country. But they were certainly guilty of today's savagery, and Comanchero guilt stained the map of Texas history for as far back as anyone could remember.

This was pay-back time!

Almost as though Lady Luck was watching over him now – after having abandoned him totally up north – a figure appeared from the sycamores, whip-lean, grey-garbed and moving with the fluid feline grace that seemed peculiar to the Comanchero. The man was leading his horse, facing away from him as Walker raised his rifle. His aim was meticulous, the pressure of his trigger finger soft as a kiss. The fierce roar of the .32 breached the sundown hush. For a moment he thought he'd missed as the Comanchero stood by his horse, head cocked to one side as though unsure if what he'd heard had been a gunshot or the timid cough of a desert lark. But then the man fell as if both legs had been cut from under him. He didn't even kick once.

At last Walker went plunging for cover. He moved lightning-fast, yet had not covered two yards before the answering shot erupted from the spring.

The yellow Sioux gelding crashed into him with stunning force, knocking him to the ground. Walker rolled violently aside as the animal fell beside him with a scream of pain, kicking wildly to free itself from the icy grip of crippled hindquarters. The enemy rifle stormed again and blood erupted from the horse's withers, gouts of bright crimson pumping in sporadic bursts, drenching Walker's shirt-front.

The horse was dying but its threshing bulk had

saved his life. Walker wriggled his way beneath the tossing head and neck, every sense honed to a razor's edge. He was acutely aware of everything; the spicy scent of the brush, the distant yipping of startled coyote, the gun echoes crashing together like boulders in an avalanche as the hidden rifleman maintained a rapid rate of fire that shredded everything within a twenty-foot radius of his target, jumping, twitching, snapping and rattling under the peppering impact of venomous lead. Coughing on dust and wiping tears from his eyes, Walker had time to understand why it was that in this moment his senses seemed suddenly sharper than had been the case in quite a time. There was nothing like seeing your life dangling by the end of a thread to sober a man real fast.

He continued to lie stone-still for a full minute until a stir of movement a short distance left of the point where the gunman had been positioned, caught his eye. He couldn't draw a bead from the position he was in. He took a chance, a big one. Jumping to his feet, he threw his rifle to his shoulder and touched off a lightning shot. This was answered by a round that whipped between his angled left arm and his body. He returned fire and the Comanchero triggered in the same instant. Walker dropped behind the horse. He levered a fresh shell into the chamber with a lightning pump of the arm, waited for the return fire that didn't come in the next minute or the ten after that.

Had it been a Cheyenne, Comanche or Sioux enemy he was trading lead bouquets with, he'd have prudently remained exactly right where he was without moving so much as a hair until full dark, and maybe well after. An Indian was born to wait you out; any buck worth his salt could lie totally motionless long enough to see grass grow. But he refused to believe a Comanchero had that sort of patience; too many exotically mixed hot bloodlines in their breed for that. His man had either slipped away or was dead, he decided, and the more he considered this notion the closer to reality it seemed to grow, until he knew what he would do.

To a chance observer, the Steve Walker who eventually rose in the deepening gloom to start up that empty slope might have appeared a very foolish man or a suicidally impatient one. He was neither. His every instinct told him there was no longer any danger for him at Hill Spring.

No shot came.

He found the dying killer sitting in the sand with his back against a sycamore. His eyes were clenched shut and he was breathing rapidly as he repeated over and over: 'Santa Maria, mother of God, spare my soul!' A vast area of dark blood, beginning to congeal, spread across the grubby white shirt-front beneath the fringed jacket. He looked about forty, was long and lean with an ashen face from which pain and terror had almost erased the lines a lifetime of evil and cruelty had etched there.

But his victor was unmoved by the pathetic sight he presented. For Walker had seen ranchos where the grey scum had raided, had smelt the sickening odour of burning flesh. He had seen fine people perish at Spanish Mountain when the raiders struck, had just today watched little Gimpy Flint, scarce bigger than a child, hurled into Eternity by the remorseless Comanchero guns.

'Heads up, scum!'

The Comanchero's eyes snapped wide and Walker's gun hammered a bullet between them.

Tobacco, snuffbox, switchblade, a broken string of pearls, a spent cartridge shell and a handful of American and Mexican coins – junk.

Walker tossed the dead man's stuff aside and crossed to the corpse of Gimpy Flint's other killer to rifle the pockets. The day was darkening and the chill of prairie, desert and plain was already cutting deep. He hunkered down. Goggling dead eyes, protruding tongue and lashings of drying blood bothered him not at all. It always felt good to squash a scorpion or blast a Comanchero. Good for Texas and good for Steve Walker, who loved this cruel land and its people, hated those who terrorized it.

High on his hate list stood the Comancheros, whose name meant literally 'those who dealt with the Comanches'. He'd always detested the breed and until recently had rated the grey horde as man's most lethal enemy in all the alien vastness that fell under the blanket-heading of the badlands. He'd maintained that attitude, in truth, until his most recent foray into the north, where he'd met something worse. Where good people had died at the hands of a mysterious, murderous enemy who even now, in vivid memory, it at times seemed hard to believe really existed, could exist.

But Walker knew they were real. Real as this man sprawled dead at his feet. There was more junk, plus a little gold-dust. Nothing to suggest that the killer had had any connection or linkage with the Comanchero band which the trail scout and his tiny party had tangled with before encountering a new kind of terror in the north-west, at a strange and hidden crater in the primitive hills which the legend-makers called Quivira.

He rose to watch the last threads of daylight draining from the western sky like blood, the rising wind humming along his hat brim and carrying on its breath the burnt resinous smells of the great valley.

In his right hand now he held the pathetic little poke of gold-dust that had cost Gimpy Flint his furtive, hard-scrabble life.

There was some sense of satisfaction in this act of retribution that he'd been able to perform. Yet deep down Walker knew the underlying reason he'd come after this pair had been in the wild hope of establishing some linkage between them and Quivira. That was the real enemy, one that was seemingly unreachable and invulnerable and would remain so unless Steve Walker was, some day, prepared to spill its secrets to the world.

And why should he ever do that?

He felt powerless to lash back at Quivira at this aimless point in his life, and so must satisfy himself with lesser kills until the pain receded and maybe he would be able to sleep without Cora Lee haunting his dreams.

But killing alone wasn't enough to ease the pain. He'd drunk the last of his whiskey, which meant it was time he was heading back for Sulphurville, where the jug was always full.

CHAPTER 2

QUIVIRA

Shattuck, storekeeper, saloonkeeper and unofficial marshal of the settlement of Sulphurville, emerged from his bar-room to take his first look at the rising sun from the store porch. The town was quiet, yet Shattuck wasn't surprised to hear himself greeted with loud familiarity from the shadows which still clung beneath the giant mesquite tree in the centre of the rough square around which the town was sprawled.

'And the top of the mornin' to you, Mr Shattuck sir!' A rattle of chains, a brief silence, then: 'Been a mighty cold night, ain't it?'

Shattuck, who was fiftyish, fattish, bull-jawed and hard-nosed in the way any businessman must be to survive out here, folded his arms and grinned toughly. He wasn't cold at all. He'd slept all night in a room with a fire in it and a plump waitress to keep him company. As Big Olan might have done had he but left the rum alone.

Big Olan never learned. Every month he came to

town it was the same. He started off drinking beers and spacing them. As time passed the intervals between drinks shortened and Big Olan grew noisier, but was still under control. But with the beer sadly affecting his will power and blocking off the corridors of memory until there wasn't even the shred of recollection of what had gone wrong on his last visit, eventually the inevitable moment came when he turned to his host, hammered on the mahogany with a fist the size of a cantaloupe, and bellowed; 'Rum, and make it a double, on the double, damn your eyes!'

It was all downhill from there. Melancholy. Paranoia. A sudden crystal-clear recollection of every single affront, real and imagined, suffered by Big Olan at the hands of this town which he had been visiting for years from his hermit hideaway in Lonesome Canyon. A disagreement. A flung punch. The smash of breaking glassware. The battle-roar of Big Olan, last of the Panhandle Swedes. Then oblivion.

Big Olan had a lump the size of a duck egg on the back of his thick skull this timid wasteland dawn, and there was a corresponding dent in the beer-bung Shattuck kept behind his bar for just such an emergency.

The troublemaker was out cold for two solid hours after the saloonkeeper snuck up on him from behind with that lethal bat.

But there was nothing like ten hours chained up to a mesquite under the frozen stars with bats crapping on a man all night long to bring him back to the land of sober reality, even if he was the last of the badland Swedes.

'Might be chill now but it's gonna be mighty hot again today,' Shattuck said at last, squinting across at the dark bulk of the Plains Hotel. 'Especially outdoors without a hat.'

The prisoner was still invisible from the store porch but he was there right enough. Sober, bat-pooped and scared.

'Marshal . . . Mr Shattuck, you wouldn't do that to a man,' he croaked. 'A man could croak.'

'Thirty dollars.'

'Hey what?'

'That's the damages you done to my place, Swede. You got that amount?'

'You know I'm done broke, Marshal.'

'I also know you're a liar. Thirty bucks, or see you at sundown, big fella. Your call.'

'But. . . . '

Olan was alone again. Soon the eastern sky reddened and the bulky outlines of the buildings took on shape and definition as life began, first to flicker weakly but soon to pulse through Sulphurville in the morning.

The prisoner spent his first waking hour cursing but was diverted upon sighting the hotel hostler hard at work cleaning down the coach, which Olan immediately realized must be the rig he'd heard roll in sometime during the night. It was a plain coach, strongly built with a black leather hardtop and sturdy axles. With nothing fast or flashy about this four-wheeler, it was plainly designed for rough country use, and the badlands could certainly provide that.

'Hey, Beau,' he called. 'Who come in overnight?'

The hostler would sooner talk than eat. He sauntered across, thoughtfully bringing along a canvas water-bag. Shattuck took his honorary law-enforcement duties seriously. With no lock-up in town, the chain-up tree provided the practical alternative. But Shattuck just chained them up and fined them. It was the responsibility of the community to provide the amenities, and if they didn't, tough. Not surprisingly, every man who ever got to spend time under the mesquite somehow managed to come up with his fine fee sooner or later.

'A big wheel and a couple of little wheels,' the hostler informed as Big Olan let the liquid gargle down his parched gullet. 'You know Damon out of Berbix?'

Big Olan belched and massaged the back of his rough head, but still managed to appear impressed.

'Chan Damon? Who don't? What's that high-pockets want here?'

'Matter of fact he's lookin' for a trail scout.'

'Him? Mr-silk-shirts-and-topper Damon? He'd croak if he ever got so far out of town that he couldn't hear the roulette wheels spinnin', wouldn't he? Where's he wanna go, man?'

'North.'

'North?'

Big Olan looked blank. North of Sulphurville was the desert and the savage heartland of the badlands, a rolling endlessness of gravel and brush and bunch grass. The private battleground of the reservation jumpers, lair of the Comanchero and a region where even a genuine desert-seasoned hardhead like himself was unlikely ever to venture either for love or gold.

And with this thought, his eyes widened.

'He don't have the gold bug, does he? Sure to God he'd be smarter'n that.'

The hostler understood what he meant. Throughout its years of parched existence the settlement of Sulphurville had heard just about every variety of treasure story, fable and gold-legend known to man. The fact that neither gold nor silver had ever been found in anything but the minutest quantities in the entire region never seemed to dim the enthusiasm of the gullible and the dreamers.

There were men in Sulphurville right now who would insist there were treasures untold just waiting to be discovered in the region, and as surely as the sun was in the sky, such starry-eyed hopefuls would tell you that it was the north-west that harboured these rich secrets.

And some daydreamers would occasionally invoke in reverential tones the mysterious name, *Quivira*.

The legend of Quivira dated back to Coronado's great expedition from Mexico in search of Cibola's Seven Cities of Gold. Those historical adventurers believed then – as many did still – that there was a place in this brutal region where even the common folk 'ate their meals off silver plates and drank from golden bowls'. That the Viceroy of Quivira journeyed the rivers in a huge canoe with forty golden oarlocks, and had subjugated all the Indian tribes into slavery in his vast mines, which produced more precious metal in just one day than any mine in America or Mexico could deliver in a year.

Gold-hunters went into the wastes searching for

Quivira and while a few returned disillusioned and empty-handed, most were never sighted again. The legend survived. But for every true believer there were a hundred realists who would have none of any of it. Numbered amongst this majority were rugged Big Olan and the hotel handyman.

'No chance,' advised the latter, turning his face to the first sunbeam to come streaking across the flatlands. 'Not Mr Damon. Matter of fact he seems to be wearing a hat I never knew he had....'

'And what hat would that be?' Big Olan was feeling better by the minute now it was full day and the fierce cold was receding.

'His Good Samaritan hat, would you believe?'

Big Olan stared at the man. Chandler Damon, renowned as the region's most flamboyant and high-rolling wheeler-dealer and entrepreneur might play many different roles from time to time in Berbix and beyond, but that of the Good Samaritan was definitely not one with which he'd ever been associated. Indeed the opposite might well be the case: instead of filling the role of the kind-hearted Biblical Samaritan, the swashbuckling Damon was more likely to be cast as the heavyweight who'd put the unfortunate traveller there.

'I reckon you're pulling my leg, Beau. Who's the big guy ever helped but himself?'

'Well, he's got this young couple with him yonder at the hotel, the Murphys. Seems her old dad is croaking up at Gun City and, like you know, that's one mighty far and risky place to get to from here. They had no luck signing up a guide in Berbix, so big-hearted Damon brung 'em up here to see if they mightn't have better luck in Sulphurville. Hey, lookit, there they be yonder now.'

Three figures strolled from the laneway adjacent to the hotel, two men and a woman. The young couple who walked hand in hand were small and slender alongside the height and shoulder-breadth of Chandler Damon. The impressively attired mover and shaker from Berbix was puffing luxuriously on his first cigar of the day as he halted to stare, first at his coach and then across to the two standing by the chain-up tree.

'Gotta go,' the hostler said. He started off, then paused. 'Say, you see any sign of Walker overnight?'

Big Olan shook his head. Then his brows lifted. 'Hey, Mr Big ain't lookin' to hire Steve, is he?'

'Reckon so. Why not?'

'You ask a man that? Glory be, he's just back from the north where he lost a good man and his gal and he's been all broody and boozing ever since. I doubt he'd take any trail job right now, never mind heading back into the north country again so soon.'

'Damon can be a mighty persuasive man,' the hostler reminded, striding away. 'And don't forget, he's loaded.'

'You reckon Steve can be bought?'

'We'll see.'

'Yeah, we'll see right enough. . . .' Big Olan lowered his rump to a gnarled and lumpy mesquite root and rattled his chains. 'When Steve gits back – if he comes back, the mood he's in – he'll more'n likely tell Mr Deep Pockets Damon to go fry. You'll see.'

'Go fry,' said Steve Walker, carefully pouring another

into his shot-glass from a brown bottle. 'I'm not hiring. Not now and not later. So *adios, amigo.*'

But Chandler Damon just smiled amiably as he rested a well-tailored elbow on the bar of Garvin's saloon and crossed one brightly polished blood-red boot over the other.

'They warned me you'd say that, Steve, and I'm sure I understand your sentiments right at this moment.' Damon spread his hands. 'You help out a young lady who just happens to be close to you, by taking her north, you run into Comanchero trouble and, tragically, you lose both your woman and a good man up there. That sort of experience would shake any man, even if he happened to be the finest and toughest trail scout in the entire wasteland, as you surely are, by God!'

Damon was laying it on with a trowel. Walker was accustomed to this kind of flattery, particularly when folks wanted to butter him up in the hope of getting him to do things he considered unwise, dangerous or downright reckless.

He sampled his drink and said nothing. The barkeep wiped the mahogany and a couple of lushes started up an argument in back in the card-room. Surrounded by the familiar sights, sounds and smells of this place he called home, the trailsman was studying his image in the mirror and assessing the damage the worst month of his life had done to him.

The gaunt and hard-jawed face of a bitter man stared back at him from the grimed glass. The face of a man who'd permitted sentiment and personal feelings to override good sense when he'd agreed to guide someone to a dangerous region he always studiously avoided, and who'd subsequently paid the price for his mistake in the hardest currency of all. Death had been his reward. Sidekick Stan Chip and lover Cora Lee dead in the Twisted Hills, leaving him wandering the wastelands alone looking for Comancheros to kill in the forlorn hope it would make him feel better.

And now, unbelievably, someone wanted him to tackle that same murderous country again.

Mr Big from Berbix had no hope. None at all.

But Chandler Damon thought differently. 'You're the only man who could take us to Gun City, Stephen....'

'Us?'

'Why, the Murphys and myself, of course.'

For the first time Walker swivelled on his stool to face the tall man directly. He was staring at the very archetype of the two-fisted go-getter who had become something of a legend in this remote section of North Texas due to his ability to get what he wanted by fair means or foul, and who somehow always managed to come up smelling like roses regardless of who else might fall by the wayside.

As a man who loved this desolate country for what it was, not for what profit he might draw from it, Walker resented the Damon breed whilst at the same time acknowledging their place in the over-all scheme of things. Men like this brought in progress, innovation and change while the Walkers of the West were content to follow the slow sure tidal-roll of the seasons and not want for much more than they already had. He knew that, deep down, Chandler Damon now regarded him as basically a loser, even if he might be a loser whose services he obviously needed.

But this barely signified. What intrigued right at this moment was the implication of what the Berbix man had just said.

'You're saying you'd be travelling personally with these people if they got a guide?' he said incredulously.

'Of course. Why so surprised, Steve?'

Walker shook his head.

'What sort of con is this, Damon? You know just as well as I do that by the time anyone travels fifty miles north of here, they're in no man's land. Nobody who respects the safety of his ass goes beyond Kaw River, and fat men with fatter bankrolls than you scarce even come even as far as Sulphurville. So why should you pretend you're ready to risk your neck just because someone comes to you with a sad story? You're lying in your teeth, and you're starting to rile me. So why don't you just get lost and go annoy someone else. There's Rogan or Dunstan or Miguel, all good men who know the badlands as good as me. Hire one of them or all of them, only get the hell off my pitch before I get riled.'

To his astonishment, Damon grabbed him by the arm.

'Walker, this might sound like horseshit to you, but I'm not the man you think. Sure, I'm a grabber and shover and I've done some things I'm not proud of in my time. But I'm still a man, still got a heart, and when these young ones came to me and begged me to help them I said to myself, "Chandler, it's time when just for once you did something for someone other than yourself", you know – turn the tables round some – stop taking and give for once.'

He released his grip and shrugged. 'I know, sounds like bulldust to me too. But it's on the level. I came here bound and determined to secure your services for this job no matter what the cost. But I also made up my mind I'd see this through with the Murphys whether you signed on or not. And I've never broken my word to myself in my life.'

Trouble was, Walker half-believed him. And while he was wearily figuring just what he might have to say or do to get this man out of his hair, the batwings opened hesitantly and they came in.

Right away, Walker knew who they were – the thin, gawky-looking young man and the skinny, pretty-faced woman clutching his hand. It could only be the Murphys, and they were dead on time. That was, if a world-weary cynic like himself believed Damon had planned this whole thing like a stage show in order that they should make an appearance right at the vital stage of the negotiations to help swing things his way.

He was peeved. But he also felt old and tired as the couple made their way for the bar and Damon jumped up with a show of surprise to perform the introductions.

A deal of windy talk followed. The Murphys would surely be 'eternally grateful' if Mr Walker would agree to guide them out to the isolated trading post at Gun City in the hope of catching up with Connie's stricken father before he passed away. In response, a sympathetic Damon felt it his duty to try and explain to the couple just why this might not be possible, in view of the fact that Walker had made a 'prior engagement' for his services.

Steve was only half-listening.

He was far more interested in what was going on inside his own skull. Namely, where he was and where he was heading in his life to give much of a damn what others might say or think.

Sure, he had told Damon to go fry, and he could stick to that.

He felt he still had a lot of drinking to do, a lot of soul-searching and guilt to deal with. He could go on rejecting offers and occasionally drift out into the desert in search of Comancheros to kill in the hope that it would make him feel better, even though only too vividly aware that the grey scum had played no more than a minor and incidental role in what had taken place in the Twisted Hills.

And no matter what he did or didn't do now, Cora Lee and Stan Chip would still be dead and gone . . . and he would still have to find a way to break out of this cocoon of self pity and take up the reins of his life again.

So why not do so now?

He hated the alacrity with which this sudden thought slotted into his thinkbox. But once lodged there he couldn't deny its pull. And with this thought came another. Maybe this was fate at work? He had suffered deeply in the north-west and had seen things there he had never spoken a word of since, for strongly held reasons of his own. The Twisted Hills lay in roughly the same wild region as Gun City. Was it possible that fate might be now plotting to lure him back there in order that he might confront his demons, show he wasn't afraid, maybe even get to overcome them in time and thus one day get to feel capable of facing Steve Walker squarely in his shaving-mirror again?

He realized belatedly that Damon was proffering a big hand.

'It's all right, Walker,' the dealer said magnanimously, every inch a man as he straightened to his full height. 'We're disappointed but we understand. Plainly you've been through more than a man should have to bear, and much as we would love to have you take us to Gun City, I can see it's too soon for you. No hard feelings?'

Walker stared at the man for a long moment. Then he turned to the young couple standing there in their cheap garments with the girl dabbing at the corner of her eye with a piece of lace.

Maybe he'd drunk too much on an empty stomach, but for a moment he was back at the mountain with the acrid stink of death in the air, and metal-clad ghosts from a bygone age were swarming about him, shrieking and howling and slashing at him with swords of gold. . . .

He blinked and he was back in Garvin's again, confronting people at risk of undertaking a dangerous journey and courting the same bloody fate as Cora Lee and Stan Chip had done, simply because they didn't have a trail scout, guide and protector to caution them and know when to warn them: 'Beyond this place there be dragons.'

With sudden impatience, he came up off his stool and brushed the proffered hand aside.

'It's hard to figure how you've done so well for yourself wheeling and dealing, Damon,' he said gruffly. 'Seems to me you give up far too easy.'

CHAPTER 3

TO THE DEATH

On the bunch's third day out from Sulphurville on the trail to Kaw River it was Rogan's turn to ride forward scout. This entailed riding far ahead of the others and keeping in touch with the trail Damon's party was following up ahead, without risking drawing too close with the possibility of being spotted by hawk-eyed Walker.

Having ridden in partnership with Steve Walker on his last fateful journey to the north in search of Cora Lee's long-lost brother, Rogan knew exactly just how fine an outdoorsman and dangerous an adversary the other was, and as a consequence was careful to take no foolish chances.

Despite the reassuring reality of a party somewhere ahead, and his own party of four tailing some ten miles in back of him, tough Rogan was nonetheless oppressively aware of the awful emptiness and the nameless dread of this desolate land.

There was nothing to see in any direction except the limitless irregular plain which each day grew brassier in colour with the withering of the buffalo grass. Sometimes at night they heard lobo wolves howling off in the blackness. Occasionally, by day, a few straggling specks of game appeared far off. From time to time the traveller found himself trailed by buzzards, those sinister harbingers of death, hopeful, leisurely, patient and grotesque. But mostly there was nothing at all to draw the eye, making it easy to concentrate upon the marks of horses and coach upon the burning earth.

Rogan was a husky man with a rocky jaw and a quick way of walking. Walker had recruited him for the Twisted Hills job, not because they were friends but because he'd considered Rogan tough enough to handle it.

So he had proved to be. The woman and Walker's second sidekick had not survived that epic journey, but Rogan had. Despite the fact that they had beaten the odds and returned to civilization alive together, Walker and Rogan were no longer friends, that was if they ever had been such. Too much had happened up there and too many questions had gone unanswered between the two for things to be any different. Rogan had not even returned to Sulphurville with Walker following the disaster but instead, with bad blood between them now, had ridden on to Berbix, a man with a goal, a secret and an important contact to seek out.

Chandler Damon.

Rogan lighted a cigarette and drew the smoke

deeply into his barrel chest. Fingering a speck of tobacco from his bottom lip, he hipped around in the saddle to check his backtrail. He nodded in satisfaction. Neither he nor his own party were raising any dust. Good. Nothing for Walker to see or get suspicious about. He covered the next ten miles in solitary silence, which provided ample opportunity for his mind to wander just as far as it liked. The hardcase scout thought a lot about the north-west and what had happened there, what had befallen him and what he speculated had happened to Walker after the Comancheros had separated them ... back in that fearsome time which none who'd lived through it would ever forget. ...

They were camped just a couple of miles due west of the looming bulk of Spanish Mountain, deep in the heart of the Twisted Hills, when Walker, standing watch, first caught wind of the Comancheros.

They broke camp fast but not fast enough. There were two small bunches of Comancheros, and when the whickering of their horses betrayed the party's position, Walker took Cora Lee and Stan Chip east while Rogan lured the killers off to the south.

This was a routine procedure for experienced trailsmen; you never tangled with Indians, Comancheros or outlaws unless under circumstances favorable to yourself.

Rogan reached the designated reunion spot to the south safely, but waited out most of the night before Walker showed up exhausted, badly cut up, alone and uncommunicative beyond relating that Chip and Cora Lee were dead, killed by the Comancheros.

They headed south and it was not until the following day that Rogan detected something, seemingly no more important than an arrowhead, embedded in the padding of Tatum's saddle. But this discovery had led to their quarrelling and eventual splitting up. The self-same 'something' which in time had taken Rogan on to Berbix, his meeting with Damon, then eventually brought him back here to the remote lands which no sane man would ever want to return to unless he had the strongest reason for doing so.

Rogan had that reason. It was wrapped in greasepaper at the bottom of the right-hand pocket of his Levis.

Darkness fell fast and hard by which time Rogan had backtracked several miles to reach his party at the canyon he had marked out as their campground *en route*. The moment he rode into the camp he knew something wasn't right. He swung down and looked around at Klein, Sisk, Dutch Annie and Achilles Cobb. He was boss of this outfit and looked it every inch.

'OK, what's cooking?' he challenged, hands on hips, light from the small, smokeless fire tinting powerful features.

'Beans,' quipped Dutch Annie, stirring the small pot on the fire. Rogan shot the leather-faced woman a cold look, then focused on the three men. He noticed Cobb and Sisk both glance in Klein's direction, nodded to himself. Klein was the one he knew least and therefore trusted less than the others.

Klein, by Rogan's assessment, could be a troublemaker with notions above himself. Time to find out.

'What you staring at Klein?' he snapped.

'Who's starin'?' Klein was lean of hip and leg but hunked heavy in the shoulders with beef. The man's face was dark and saturnine. He fancied himself as a brawler and carried a big knife in the back of his gunbelt.

'You forgot to say *sir*,' Rogan pushed.

Klein flushed.

'What's eatin' you, Rogan? You're gone all day and you come back all proddy and ornery.'

'You've got something cooking, mister. I've scented it all along. I've seen you confabbing with the others when you thought I wasn't looking. I don't like geezers talking behind my back. If you got something on your mind, out with it.'

'OK,' Klein retorted. 'What's on my mind is you, Rogan, you and Damon. You sign us up for this job of work but you don't tell us what it's all about. You're keepin' it to yourselves, and that just don't suit. Travellin' this spook country's tough enough even when a man knows why he's here and what he's doin', but it's a mighty sight worse when you're left in the dark.'

The man paused to gesture northwards.

'What's waitin' us up there? Man hears all sorts of talk about this durned Quivira. And that's where Damon's makin', ain't it?'

Rogan stood lazily with his weight on one hip, peeling off his riding-gloves. This was a man of many parts, some impressive, others less so. He'd qualified to join Steve Walker's doomed search for Cora Lee's brother on the basis of his status as a trailsman in other places, but chiefly due to his reputation as a hard man, hard enough, as he was to prove, to survive a murderous encounter with the Comancheros at Quivira. Chandler Damon appreciated this quality in Rogan and had had no hesitation in placing him in charge of his back-up bunch whose job it was to trail the Gun City-bound party without Walker being aware of it. He suspected Dutch Annie, Cobb and Sisk might be happy enough to accept his authority, but ox-shouldered Klein had proven testy bordering on insolent from the outset.

Right now it sounded a whole heap to Rogan's ear as if the towering Panhandler was throwing down some kind of a challenge.

He said softly; 'Mr Damon's gonna tell us what it's all about when we get there. OK?'

'No it ain't OK.' Klein glanced round for support from his three companions. But suddenly it seemed his eye was infected by ptomaine; nobody wanted to catch it. He flushed and socked a fist into his palm with a smack as he approached the fire. 'It ain't OK, Rogan, on account of we know you went to the big man first off when you come to Berbix after quittin' Walker. It had to be whatever you told him that got him so fired up about ridin' north. Now it suits you to make out you're just one of the boys followin' orders, but we ain't buyin' it.' He jabbed a long forefinger at the centre of Rogan's barrel chest. 'Time we knew why, and you're goin' to tell us.'

Rogan's face didn't alter its expression. Inside it

was different. No guessing whether this was a serious challenge any longer. This was the real McCoy.

'Sorry you see things that way, big fella,' he said casually. Then his right shoulder dipped and his hand swept up full of Colt .45. 'OK, pal, shuck the shooter.'

'You dirty son of a whore—' Klein began but broke off when Rogan cocked the piece with an ominous click. His face engorged with fury as the others looked on in frozen silence; he plucked his sidearm from its scabbard and hurled it to the ground. 'There you go. Somehow I had you figured as the kind of scumsucker who'd want the odds all his own way before he had the guts to make a play. So what are you gonna do? Kill me for askin' what any man has a right to know? You want me to grovel? You'll wait until hell freezes over.'

There was a thud as Rogan's Colt hit the buffalo grass close by Klein's. Klein stared uncomprehendingly, affording Rogan time to close the distance separating them in three smooth strides.

'Can't have gunplay in case we attract attention,' he said firmly. 'But this is a war zone and we gotta have discipline or we're done for, pal.'

The punch he threw so fast crunched into Klein's teeth and jolted the bigger man back on his heels. He was dazed for a moment but not longer. Something akin to triumph glittered in the Panhandler's agate eyes as he spat blood and slipped into a boxer's crouch.

'You just made the biggest mistake of your life, Damon's boy!' he hissed. And charged.

Klein was good.

Rogan realized this in the first handful of seconds that saw him on the defensive, ducking whistling hooks and ripping undercuts that had the stamp of the pro prizefighter in their sledgehammer power and speed of reflex. Several blows found their target, but this was where Rogan's prime talent manifested itself. The man was genuinely teak-tough and at his most dangerous when stacked up against a formidable adversary. He soaked up three solid hits in a row in order to position himself for one pistoning rip to the solar plexus. But what a blow it was. Klein looked like a man who feared he'd been cut in half as he dropped protective elbows to his guts and backed up, only to have Rogan come crowding in now, hurling them from everywhere.

'You're not saying much now, Klein,' he panted. 'How come? Minute back we couldn't shut you up.' He feinted at the brow then sledged a brutal straight right to the heart. 'Don't like the arrangement, big fella? Heck, you didn't know how good you had it, did you? This is how bad it can get, and it'll get worse because I get a real charge trimming nothings like you down to your rightful pygmy size. Here comes the axe again.'

Stung more by the taunting than the punishment he was absorbing, Klein fought back for a time. For several brutal minutes the combatants surged to and fro, until Rogan stepped into a punch he didn't see and buckled at the knees. With a roar of triumph, Klein suddenly seized his left arm and threw him clear over his back in a flying mare. Rogan hit the ground with a thud and Klein fell upon him, a knee pistoning into his mid section and an elbow crashing across his chin. Was Rogan all through?

The hard man provided the answer with a jolting head butt that split Klein's forehead. Blood gushed, and as the big man rolled off him, Rogan kicked him in the groin. Klein's hand vanished behind him and reappeared, flashing steel. Rogan had forgotten the big knife!

He sustained a long gash clear across his chest in the savage fight-wrestle that churned up the dust and saw the little fire kicked to pieces. Then a bloody-faced Klein had the knife-point bearing down on Rogan's taut throat.

'You dirty mongrel bastard, Rogan!' he almost sobbed. 'I'm gonna slit you crotch-to-Christmas and feed your entrails to the coyotes.'

Klein was talking when he should have been cutting. Rogan thudded a knee into Klein's short ribs, and when the bigger man groaned and sagged, he craned his head forward and sank his teeth deep into the tendons of the hand clutching the blade, biting to the bone. Klein screamed and the knife fell upon Rogan's heaving chest. He snatched it up and drove the blade into the heart, twisting it savagely as it went in all the way to the hilt. Their eyes blazed into one another's until Klein's filmed over, and Rogan was able to heave the body off him as though it no longer had any weight or substance.

When the others rushed to his aid, he armed them away and got to his feet with a tremendous act of will, standing swaying in the faint starlight.

'Klein's mistake was that he thought he was something,' he said with the arrogant assurance of the victor. 'But I rounded him up in the back dives of Berbix just like I did with the rest of you.' He paused to catch his breath and wipe a dead man's blood from his face. 'You signed on for a tough job on big dough, no questions asked until me and Damon are ready to tell you. Klein decided the arrangement didn't suit, now there'll be no big pay-day for him. So anybody else who can't take the hard going, this is your last chance to head back. My way or the highway, *amigos*. What's it gonna be?'

Dawn light would find four riders pushing north along the tracks left by Walker's party as the plainslands' first buzzards came gliding up from the south. They'd respected him even before the fight: Dutch Annie, Achilles Cobb and Sisk. Now they also feared him. The badlands depressed their spirits while gory tales of Comancheros and bizarre Quivira legends, which all had heard before, began to take on enormous significance out here. The trio, hardcases all, rode tightly together in back of Rogan's wide-shouldered figure in the saddle, finding strength in unity, feeling that now they were earning every cent Damon was paying for their services.

They continued their long eerie journey as though traversing this ghastly landscape beneath a cloud of pending doom. But not one had turned back, nor would they. For, despite the secrecy of Damon and Rogan, by one means or another each outlaw had caught the faintest whiff of a pot of gold at the end of this badlands rainbow. The late Klein had all but convinced them that nothing less than the prospect of great gain – possibly some mighty treasure-trove – could have tempted a high-roller like Damon to put his life on the line by venturing into the haunted north.

Crossing the low Kaw River mid-afternoon beneath a savage sun felt like passing into the unknown. There were no maps of what lay ahead and the party had to rely on Rogan's local knowledge to inform them, when just on sundown a tiny distant hump they could barely see rose above the northern horizon, that they were looking at the highest crest of the fabled Spanish Mountain.

They stared at one another in awe. Few people ever dared venture far enough out here to get to glimpse Quivira.

Silence. Cold sweat. The ashy taste of danger.

Walker barely seemed to breathe as he pressed his rangy body back into the natural recess in the clay wall of this unnamed canyon. His vision blocked on either side, he stared down at the sunwashed patch of canyon floor directly before him in the hope that a shadow might be cast to alert him which way the danger was approaching.

It had to be danger.

Upon leaving the others to search for water in the canyon, he'd issued strict instructions that nobody was to quit the camp. So it could only be an enemy horse he'd heard here. But what shape he might take, whether paint-daubed Comanche, murderous desert rat or unwashed Comanchero, there was no guessing. Perhaps it could even be those strange warriors from the crater hidden high in the mountain.

Thought of their attackers in that bloody encounter which had taken place not twenty miles from where he now stood, still chilled him. Another man in his position might have been readily prepared to tab them Conquistadores, Coronadans or simply the Spanish. But Steve Walker was a level-headed trailsman of the great south-west, always slow to hang a fanciful or fantastic name on a thing until he'd exhausted the logical possibilities. True, in the painful weeks since he'd lost two friends and barely escaped the Twisted Hills with his life, he'd found himself unable to come up with any logical explanation of what he'd encountered. The one given was, that whoever or whatever the mystery people up there might be, they were as lethal an enemy as any to be found in the badlands. He stiffened at the sound of a walking horse. Moments later the flung shadow of horse and rider fell across his narrow patch of floor before the fissure. Walker's Colt was levelled and cocked as the head of a familiar looking grey pony appeared, the weapon slowly coming down only when he found himself staring at an unsuspecting Connie Murphy.

The girl almost swooned with fright when he thrust himself forward to seize the grey's headstall.

'What the hell do you think you're doing?' He was mad as the devil. Any trail scout hated to have his orders flouted; that was how people got killed.

He simmered down when the woman burst into

tears. She was skinny, freckled and pretty in a country kind of way. And she was scared. She'd been scared even before quitting Sulphurville.

'It's all right,' Walker muttered, patting her arm. 'But just where did you think you were going?'

'Back,' she blubbered. 'This place terrifies me, Mr Walker, I can't stand it any longer.'

'What about your dying daddy in Gun City?'

She avoided his gaze as she wiped tears from freckled cheeks

'I'm sorry,' she sniffed. She pulled the grey's head around. 'I'd better get back, hadn't I.'

'Sounds like a good idea.'

Trailing her back up canyon, Walker massaged his jaw and his frown cut deep. There was something odd about the Murphys from Berbix, he decided. Somehow they just didn't weigh up like a girl fretting for her dying father, and a husband with nothing better to do than risk his neck helping her cross the big nowhere to get to his side. More like a none-too-smart young fellow and his young bride finding out that wedded bliss wasn't everything it was cracked up to be, if he were any judge.

As for Damon the philanthropist, he was finding him even less reassuring than the others, as time passed. But the big man's cash wasn't something he could question, and Walker was still convinced he'd made the right decision in agreeing to escort the party through to Gun City. Like a man stove up in a bad horse accident, he'd needed to climb back in the saddle again. He'd always been something of an idealist about his life and especially about this country, and now he was back in the real wilds he could feel the pain was easing and everything seemed to be falling back into place.

They found Bill Murphy and Damon scouring the brush surrounding the camp for the missing girl. Damon and Murphy seemed ready to tie into Connie, but Walker wasn't having any of this.

'She got spooked and she wanted out,' he stated firmly, handing her down from her pony. 'Simple as that. Could happen to any one of us, so let's hear no more about it.'

Murphy folded up immediately, slipping his arm around his wife's shoulders and giving her a reassuring squeeze. But Damon was not much for taking orders, as he'd demonstrated several times during their travels.

'You could smile when you talk like that, Walker,' he said, leaning against the rear baggage-rack of his coach.

Walker caught the edge to the words but did not react.

'We're getting low on water,' he said. 'But there's a spring about seven – eight miles north-west.'

'What's wrong with due north?' Damon challenged.

'That'd take us off our trail towards the mountain.'

'But you told me last night there's water at the mountain.'

'I don't mean to go near the mountain.'

'Who's paying for this waltz? I say let's get to the mountain, water up then pick up our trail north-west again.' Damon held up a hand palm forward as Walker made to protest. 'I know, I know, you don't like the mountain. But I want to see it and I'm paying your wages, mister. Do I make myself clear?'

Walker's eyes narrowed. The Chandler Damon he'd encountered briefly in Berbix once or twice in the past had been a flamboyant figure surrounded by stooges, pretty women and a plush life style. The Sulphurville Damon had been somewhat different, amiable, impressive and exuding a new-found compassion for his fellow man. But this wasteland Damon was one tough *hombre* with a knack for letting you know he was boss of this outfit in just about everything he said and did.

Damon was alone without his usual retinue of bodyguards and yes-men out here, yet acted exactly as if they were ranked up right behind him. Curious, that. Maybe as an individual the man was far tougher and gutsier than Walker had given him credit for.

He stared north. The mountain loomed. He managed to suppress the bad memories easily enough. No option. For he was being paid to do a job of work, as his employer had just reminded him.

Walking to his horse, he caught Rogan's eye and pointed north.

He didn't catch Damon's smile, but it was really something to see. Like the smile of a tiger.

CHAPTER 4

OUT OF THE PAST

The moon was high and clear.

Walker lowered his bottle and waited for the whiskey to hit his guts. He should have known that it would strike him once they got here – the guilt, the sense of loss, the pain. It had been somewhere close to this spot that they'd made camp on the south-west slopes of the rugged mountain. When he'd fled through the night with his sidekick and his girl with the stink of Comanchero killers in the air, with Rogan hammering off away south to divert the enemy. Now he was back, alive and strong but Stan and Cora Lee were long gone. And why?

Because they'd put their trust in Steve Walker. That was why – or leastwise so the whiskey was telling him.

So, what's your response, Walker? quizzed an inner voice. How do you plan to handle this burden you're carrying? Get drunk and maybe lose your second party in as many weeks? That'll solve everything, won't it.

He stoppered the bottle with an air of finality but doubted he really meant it. It had taken losing the girl he loved in the worst way imaginable to make him realize just how much his woman had meant to him. A man needed whiskey to ease that kind of pain.

He swung his head sharply at the sound of a horse, to see Damon riding up from the remuda. Walker came to his feet in one lithe motion, threw up his arm.

'Just where the hell do you think you're going, Damon?'

The big man reined in.

'What's it look like? I'm taking a ride.'

Walker cursed. 'You're taking a ride?' he mimicked. 'Just like that? Are you out of your head, man? Nobody rides alone out here by daylight much less by night. There are a hundred ways you could get killed—'

'Relax, trail boss. Just because you got mauled over up here doesn't mean lightning will strike twice in the one place.' Damon made an expansive gesture which encompassed brooding mountain and thicket-covered foothills. 'It's a mighty night, I feel like a kid again and I'm going to enjoy it while I can in case I wake up tomorrow an old man.'

'You are loco!'

'Better take another shot of hooch, mister. You sound like a man whose nerve is cracking. Back in an hour or two. *Hasta la vista.*'

Damon was a picture of bravado as he swung wide

round the unharnessed coach, threw a wave at the startled figures close by, then vanished southward into the brush.

Yet the moment the campground was cut off from his sight, the big man's feigned grin vanished as though it had never existed. Throughout his prosperous career Berbix's Mister Big had been involved in many a chancy situation. He'd traded with Indians who had human scalps hanging from their belts, done deals with outlaws whose faces were plastered on wanted dodgers across Texas. In his time he'd been shot at, poisoned and had gone to bed with painted women who carried stilettos in their garters.

But this job was really scary. And by the time his horse carried him clear of the first stand of mesquite he was riding fast with a chill running down his spine like ice-water.

Although Damon knew exactly what he was doing and where he was headed, that wasn't enough to steady his nerves. He could play it tough better than most, and it was the role he liked best. But it was little more than that. Just role-playing. Deep down Chandler Damon was soft-centred. But being rich and successful he could mostly afford to hire genuinely tough people to be brave on his behalf. That was how he operated in Berbix and it was no different out here at the tip-ass end of civilization. He still had his support, even out here. Only thing, tonight he must cover a considerable piece of eerie and moon-haunted distance alone before he would link up with it.

But he'd memorized the directions Rogan had

supplied him with down to the last detail. Rogan was good at that sort of thing, setting things up, dishing up information, listing the dangers. In truth, that hardnose was good at just about anything he took on, which was a large part of the reason why Damon had at least half-swallowed his wild story about the gold, and agreed to cut himself in on his proposition.

Trouble with a man like that, though, was that a man never knew just how far he could trust him. Sure, Rogan had everything to gain and nothing to lose by playing it straight with him out here. But there was the man's reputation to consider. Rogan just wasn't regarded as the best with fists, guns or anything that might be handy. His reputation extended to the double cross, the sell-out, the con and outright betrayal.

And wasn't it a fact that, right now, Rogan was in the middle of using a former trail partner, maybe a man who'd even once been a friend, in Walker?

He ran a finger around his collar. Although Rogan was the bragging swaggering extrovert of that former partnership, there was something about Walker that told you he was not a man you'd want coming after you for any reason.

And who could tell how this deal might play out? What if he wound up with Walker on his tail – maybe Rogan as well, if the Damon talent for the double-cross should rear its ugly head?

'The hell with it!' he said aloud. 'You're the brains, they've only the muscle. Quit spooking yourself and get on with it, man.'

He was soon guiding the horse through coarse

thornbrush – which Rogan had noted on his mud map. It wasn't long before he sighted the yellow rock outcrop passing by on his right, ahead the dry creekbed wound crookedly away south.

He followed the dead watercourse for several miles without incident until, with a huge sigh of relief, he glimpsed the landmark lightning-struck dead tree, all ghostly white in the moonlight directly ahead.

He felt freshly reassured that he'd made a wise decision in going into partnership with Rogan when the familiar broad-shouldered figure swaggered into clear view and called a greeting just as casually and calmly as if they were meeting up in Berbix on Sundown Street.

'Walker's still drinking?' Rogan sounded surprised. 'That ain't his usual style even in town, let alone on the trail.'

'You're talking about the old Walker,' Damon replied, lighting his second cigar with a flourish. 'They warned me in Sulphurville he's been giving the syrup a nice old nudge ever since you and him got back. His girl, so they say.'

'Yeah, that Cora Lee was sure some woman. . . .'

'Had your eye on her yourself, I wouldn't doubt?'

'You loco? Would I do that to a pard?'

'Ex-pard, isn't it?'

'Well, nothing lasts for ever. Old Steve, he's sure a man to ride the river with. But, hell, that joker takes everything too blamed serious. Sometimes being around him is like going to church. You know?

Everything's gotta be straight down the line, honest and squeaky clean.' He spread his hands. 'I mean, who the hell lives like that anyway?'

'There could be something to be said for those old-fashioned values.' Damon paused, his expression quizzical. 'You wouldn't let down a partner, would you?'

'Why do you say that? Has Walker been talking to you. . . ?' Rogan began, then broke off. 'Hey! You're talking about our deal now, ain't you? Yours and mine.' He laughed reassuringly. 'You got nothing to worry about, big man.' He flung his arms wide in an expansive gesture. 'This deal is so huge there ain't gonna be no need for nobody to think about getting greedy and maybe cutting someone else out. There'll be plenty for everybody. Ain't that so . . . partner?'

'Hope so.'

Rogan clapped him on the shoulders with a laugh. It was just a pat yet Damon staggered. Rogan had the strength of a working bullock.

'Hope so? You know so,' Rogan insisted. He was sober in an instant. 'But how about our plan, eh, partner? Is it working like clockwork, or ain't it?'

'You've done fine, Rogan, just fine,' Damon assured generously. He was glancing across at the others hunched over a tiny fire at the base of the granite feature known as Sentinel Rock. 'Not even Walker had a notion you were trailing us, and he's got eyes in the back of his head. Maybe that's a sign about how far he's slipped. . . .'

Rogan's eyes hardened.

'It's a sign of what a sweet job I've done of tailing

you, that's what it's a sign of. But I agree that old Steve has slipped plenty since the last time I was riding with him.

'He had balls once but he ain't reliable now. Which means we might find ourselves having to depend on every other man we've got before this turkey-shoot is over. And woman, if that's what Dutch Annie is.' Rogan nodded his big head emphatically. 'We still don't know exactly what breed of trouble Walker ran into here that night, but whatever it was it cost him dear and shook him up real good. But we're five strong here. Plus you, that should still give us enough firepower if that's what we're going to need to come up trumps. Right?'

Damon studied this man who had become his unlikely partner in what was shaping up as the epic enterprise of his high-rolling career.

Rogan had been no more than a casual acquaintance before this operation, just another of those rugged, nail-hard characters living on the shady side of the street, but with enough talent and savvy to ensure he made a good living and kept out of the clutches of the law. A man with strengths and weaknesses who might just as easily wind up butchered in some alley, as rich and successful, depending on Lady Luck.

That capricious lady had beamed warmly upon Rogan the day she saved his life in the deadly clash with the Comancheros here in the Twisted Hills, and he'd demonstrated how smart he was when he eschewed returning to Sulphurville with a shattered Walker, but instead rode straight on to Berbix to rap on Chandler

Damon's door with a solid gold arrowhead.

Canny Rogan had realized he'd stumbled on to something momentous from the moment he plucked that arrowhead out of the padding of Walker's saddle, right on this very spot at first light long weeks ago following their separate escapes from the Comancheros. So excited had he been, in fact, that he'd flatly refused to turn the piece over to Walker, which had almost touched off a showdown between the two scouts. The instant Rogan realized both that the arrowhead was indeed fashioned from solid gold and that Walker was deliberately refusing to offer any sort of explanation concerning how and where he'd come by it, Rogan's curiosity had been ignited.

Intuitively he was connecting everything he'd ever heard about the epic journey of Coronado's gold-seekers through these regions, and the hard-to-swallow fables of lost cities and great treasures beyond price – legends which had haunted this remote land for longer than anyone remembered. Until at last it dawned upon him that he, rough-edged Joe Rogan, had been singled out by Lady Luck to lift the veil that had enshrouded the mystery of Quivira and maybe get to make himself obscenely rich and famous in the process.

He could live with that.

A voice floated down from atop Sentinel Rock.

'Looks like weather blowin' up from the south, Rogan!'

Rogan dismissed Cobb's warning with an impatient gesture. Typhoons could rage and all the badland rivers fill and burst their banks for all he cared. All that signified right now was for him to hear Damon explain how the last hand in this high-stake game was to be played out.

But Damon would not be hurried. It was essential at this stage for him to make a full and measured review of the situation and his plans in order to ensure he'd overlooked nothing before launching himself into the next and most vital stage of operations.

'Let me see it again,' he demanded through a haze of cigar smoke.

Rogan's hand shook just a little as he drew the oilcloth-wrapped object from his pocket and handed it across. Turning his broad back on Dutch Annie and Sisk, who were pretending to be currying the horses to cover their interest, Damon unwrapped the small package. The arrowhead lay slender and golden in his palm.

His smile was wide and glitter-eyed.

His initial response to the treasure Rogan had brought to him at Berbix some time ago had been to solicit the professional services of Berbix's assayer, who happened also to be a geologist and local historian of considerable note. The expert's reaction had been one of amazed excitement. He was an avid student of Coronado's American journeys, was steeped in such detailed matters pertaining to it as modes of transport, dates, maps, significant events, military modes, dress, protocols, communications and armaments. There was no doubt in his mind that the configuration of the arrowhead and the manner in which it had been moulded established it as of authentic Mexican and Spanish origin in every aspect but that of age. The assayer was convinced that the object was quite new, and was simply busting to know how Damon had come by it.

Instead of setting the fellow's curiosity to rest Damon had pumped him for every piece of knowledge he had of Coronado's journeys across the deserts and badlands, then paid him his fee and showed him the door.

From that moment on the partnership of Damon and Rogan was rock-solid reality. They would return to the Twisted Hills together, yet they agreed that such an expedition would require careful planning. For many a man had searched for Quivira all across north-west Texas and New Mexico and never returned.

It took little time for them to agree that Steve Walker was pivotal to the entire affair. He alone knew how and under what circumstances he'd apparently had a solid gold arrow fired at him. But Walker wasn't talking at that time. He was back in Sulphurville with no mention of any gold, sheeting blame for the Twisted Hills disaster squarely at the feet of the Comancheros – an explanation everyone swallowed whole with the exception of the two men in Berbix who knew better.

Damon and Rogan were still mystified about Walker's total lack of interest in that chunk of precious metal which Rogan had dug out of his saddle. He'd seemed so shattered by grief and guilt at the time that nothing really signified but drifting and drinking.

But the scout's mood had in no way delayed Damon's mapping out a plan, first to lure an unsuspecting 'horse' – Walker – back to the mountain, and then both to lead him to the water and force him to drink.

'Hey!' Rogan said, snapping his fingers. 'You still with me?'

Damon rose and returned the package; Rogan wouldn't allow it out of his sight. Damon swung his big head at the sound of distant thunder and felt a cold wind pressing against his back as it came swirling through tortured trees and brush.

'He's an odd mix, that scouting man,' he stated abruptly as though aware Rogan would know whom he was talking about. 'I've studied him at close quarters over the best part of a week and I still don't have him figured as clearly as I'd like.' He paused with a puzzled frown. 'Is he actually in love with this hell on earth, or is that just some kind of front?'

'It's the real thing.' Rogan grimaced as he gazed around at the haunted landscape lying beneath an icy moon. 'Claims it's the last unspoiled wilderness in the whole country, and sees it as his duty to keep it that way.'

He paused and tapped his temple. 'Wild Injuns, free-ranging outlaws, a playground for Comancheros and a climate that'd kill a rattler ... yet Walker thinks it's paradise. A little tetched if you ask me, but mortal tough. We better not overlook that factor when it comes time for us to figure how to make Steve Walker do something he sure as shooting won't want to do.'

'I suppose . . .' Damon mused thoughtfully, 'that the only reason that makes sense of Walker's clamming up about our artefact is that if he's stumbled on to some big find – as we figure. If that's the case then it's likely he's got his own plans to come back, maybe even on this expedition, and scoop it all up into his . . .' He broke off with a frown. 'Why are you shaking your head?'

'Guess I forgot to tell you.'

'Tell me what?'

'He hates gold.'

'Are you loco? Nobody hates gold.'

'Walker does. His folks died in a miners' riot in New Mexico when he was a kid, and since then he sees gold and mining as the root of all evil.' Rogan snorted. 'Like I say, a little tetched.' He sobered, steadying himself against the strengthening gusts. 'Looks like real weather coming in. Seems to me we oughta be doing more riding and less jawing, partner.'

'You're right,' Damon agreed, turning to his horse. 'Tell them to break camp. I'll tell you how we'll go about things as we ride.'

The thunderstorm caught them before they'd covered a mile, lightning-riddled skies delivering up a lashing rain that swept across the darkened landscape, beating an incessant tattoo on hatbrim and slicker and cutting visibility to a few yards.

But Rogan the trailsman knew the route and led

them unerringly across quickly filling creeks and gully-washes and on into the wooded foothills where lightning flashes silhouetted the brooding bulk of the mountain and occasionally illuminated the antelope pad winding its way to Damon's campsite.

Where they found the Murphys huddled in the coach.

The couple reacted with some alarm at the jarring sight of three of Berbix's more notorious citizens suddenly showing up unheralded in the company of Rogan and Damon. Their reaction was ignored by a puzzled Damon and a scowling Rogan as they heeled their horses about the campsite, looking for Walker.

'Where the hell is he?' Rogan demanded of the couple, reining in alongside the rig again. 'Where's Steve?'

They had no idea. One moment he'd been there, the next he was gone. They hadn't seen him in two hours, and they were scared.

A look of suspicion passed between the grim-faced partners. This didn't sound good. Not good at all.

Comancheros!

He thought he could still smell them here by the scrub-oak, that sickly, feral body stink as pungent and foul as it had been the night when the three of them had paused here to get their bearings, Steve Walker, Stan Chip and Cora Lee. He could feel his neck-hair bristle and lift even as the rational part of his mind was reassuring him there were no Comancheros. Not here by the oakscrub, nor in the foothills nor any place within a day's journey of Quivira.

He knew his reaction was no more than emotion evoked by his return to the place where he'd held Cora Lee's hand for the last time before the real nightmare began. Standing hatless in the thinning rain as the storm lashed its way off into the south, Walker stared back west, in the direction he'd come. Back where he'd left tenderfeet unprotected as he'd never done in his long career, surrendered his responsibilities with a bottle in his fist – again a career first for Steve Walker of Sulphurville.

He shuddered.

Everything he was doing here was out of character. It might have been all right had Damon not insisted they visit the Twisted Hills, and had not the rush of bitter memories that the place evoked driven him to ease the pain with whiskey. It had been too soon to come back, he knew now. But once here, within a mile of where it had all happened, he'd been impelled to revisit the scene of the disaster, to torture himself by reliving every moment. The wind moaning in the oakscrub now was Chip's mortal cry as a Comanchero bullet cut him down. And hand-in-hand, he and Coral Lee were rushing away through the blackness, running and stumbling until the earth gave way beneath them and they were running on the air.

Somehow he managed to break her fall. They could not hear the enemy now but they continued to run, a darkness in the gloom ahead suggesting some sort of shelter. Plunging into the cavern, they found it actually gave on to a twisting tunnel, which they followed in almost total darkness until they were suddenly under open skies again, on a strip of grassy sward in what appeared to be a giant, high-walled basin ringed by yellow cliffs ... with strange lights flickering on the dark floor somewhere below.

Then came the attack.

They appeared from nowhere, alien, armour-plated figures with starlight gleaming off breastplates, halberds, rapiers and helmets, some mounted but most afoot, howling in Spanish and hacking at them savagely until Walker's .45 snarled again and again and they began to fall.

No reason here, just mindless savagery that continued until the couple were separated. Then, as a desperate Walker attempted to blast his way through to reach Cora Lee's side, he saw the figure rush at her, saw the sword strike her slender body and heard her last cry as she vanished over the sheer drop to plummet towards the lights below.

He went crazy at that point as three horsemen, all in gleaming gold armour, attempted to run him down. He backed himself into a corner formed by sturdy man-made barricades, ducking desperately as a thrumming arrow missed his head by a hair's breadth.

His .45s exploded and a hard-riding figure curved backwards in his saddle with both hands clapped to his forehead, blood squeezing through his fingers. Walker barely had time to fling himself over the barricade before the next attacker was upon him, hacking at him with a shimmering sword, screaming in Spanish. Walker parried a sword-thrust with his left-hand gun, shoved the other into the rider's guts and gave him three up close.

The dead man fell like a stone and and a desperate scout vaulted the barricade, hit ground, bounced and vaulted into the empty saddle before the terrified horse could back away.

He triggered until his guns ran empty, the whole scene wreathed in gunsmoke and made hideous by the screams of the dying and the enraged.

The maw of the natural tunnel loomed.

He used his spurs cruelly and was soon clattering back through the tunnel with arrows whistling by his ears and the crack of some ancient firearm filling the darkness with head-splitting echoes.

He escaped because they didn't come after him, and so survived to make his rendezvous with Rogan at Sentinel Rock after having lashed his way past this giant old tree which swayed above him now.

He stared eastwards, emotion constricting his throat as he found himself barely able to distinguish against the dim light of the first stars following the storm the cliff wall which barred the way to the crater.

There was nothing for him here. What had taken place that night had been bewildering, inexplicable, fantastic, and a black tragedy.

But he would let it lie.

Cora Lee was gone. He had kept his secret of the amazing things which he had seen and survived, yet still only half-believed, and that would be the end of it. Have another drink and get over it, Walker. Take Damon and the couple on to Gun City tomorrow and put her out of your mind . . . along with warriors in golden armour who'd emerged out of the mists of history to bring you grief and drive you crazy. . . .

With a jerky action, he lifted the bottle to his lips, but halted when he caught the smell of the liquor. For a moment he stared at the bottle in surprise and something like relief. It disgusted him. His face twisting with revulsion, he hurled the whiskey from him with all his strength, the sound of it smashing to pieces against the leaning scrub-oak trunk like a tinkling bell signalling the close of something, proclaiming the period point.

The melancholy slowly lifted as he rode. By nature and design this was a man of action and disciplined habits to whom the role of the victim and sufferer was alien. He'd done his hurting, kept his own counsel, finished his drinking and it was time to go forward and be what he would always be while he still had the strength and the love of the cruel beauty of this land to sustain him. He was Steve Walker, trail scout – once again.

The horse responded to his touch now as the night wind cleansed his skull of the last of the liquor fumes, and he felt a renewed sense of responsibility kick in. Of course, he told himself, he would not have left the Murphys unprotected had he believed them to be in the slightest danger. Still, he would feel one hell of a lot better when he rode into camp and saw them safe and sound.

Which he did.

The two of them were seated on a deadfall, attempting to relight the fire which had been doused by the thunderstorm. They looked up at him, all pale and wan-looking, and Walker responded with a grin of pure relief as he reined in.

'Some blow, eh?' He jerked a thumb as he swung down. 'Needed to check on the creeks. Er, everything OK here? Damon not back yet?'

They didn't answer. Their eyes were stretched wide and he realized that both of them appeared quite pale. Frowning in puzzlement, Walker was about to speak when the sound of the coach door creaking open brought him swinging about sharply, hand dropping to gunbutt.

'Damon!' he grated as the big man alighted by the foot-rests. 'Where...?' He stopped as the second man appeared, his brows lifting in surprise as he identified the swaggering muscular figure of Rogan. The sixshooter in his former partner Rogan's right hand was angled casually at the ground as he jumped down and called: 'OK, you can show yourselves now!'

The click of cocking weaponry from directly in back of him warned Walker of big trouble even before he whirled on the balls of his feet to see them emerging from the wet brush. He was staring at three strangers, two men and a female with *pistolas* in their fists and the outlaw stink coming off them like rotting trash.

The sudden quiet was so deep it made his ears ache.

CHAPTER 5

TERROR DAWN

'Believe it or not, Steve,' Damon stated amiably, 'you are looking at one of the hardest men in this country to sell on any stripe of treasure-story, lost gold-mine mystery or buried-loot scam in the entire state of Texas. I mean, as an entrepreneur and a man with a dollar, I have them coming to me in droves. At times, in truth, I feel as though I need to hire an extra man whose sole job would be to protect me from *hombres* who not only think they can make me a million but are prepared to guarantee it if only I'd ante up with a little assistance and a big grubstake to help them go grab some fortune just waiting to be taken. Understand what I'm saying?'

No response.

Walker now occupied the deadfall along with the Murphys, encircled by hard-faced people with guns. He'd been disarmed but not hurt. Not yet. He fixed a cold eye on Rogan, who was smirking in the background. The man winked and held up the arrowhead. Then he shrugged his shoulders high and spread his hands as if apologetic, which was something he never was.

'What I'm saying,' Damon continued in the same sincere, conversational tone, 'is that it really takes something special to grab this old pro's attention. But Rogan managed it. Right, Joe?'

Rogan flipped him the arrowhead, which Damon caught deftly. Cobb had got the fire going, and Damon held the object above the flames between thumb and forefinger to catch the light.

'Of course, anybody could come by one of these if he really wanted, I guess,' he went on. 'Hell, a con man might outlay for a couple of ounces of pure yellow and have a goldsmith whip up something like this as a prop to hang a good con story on.' He paused. 'But when the assayer checked this out for me and assured me it was fashioned in a style unique to seventeenth-century Mexican armourers and craftsmen – he got quite excited about it as a matter of fact – that was when I really started pricking my ears.' He put on a smile. 'You can understand why, of course.'

He made an expansive gesture. 'Quivira, the city of gold. Stories have been drifting about it for God knows how long. But everyone reckoned it was just that, a windy yarn like most gold stories are. But this arrowhead was real, so naturally I had to sit Rogan down and get to hear how he came by it. Exactly.'

A gust of wind hurried across the clearing. Connie Murphy dabbed at her eyes. Dutch Annie, who was now honing a wicked-looking knife on the thigh of her leather riding-skirt, watched Walker speculatively through yellow eyes.

'You're not saying much, Steve,' Damon remarked after a silence.

That was true enough. His shock had quickly passed to be replaced by red rage. Piece by piece now he was being fed the whole story. The story of the cross, the con, the deception. But he didn't have to hear it all to realize that this set-up could only amount to the very worst: Damon's smirking self-assurance, the trio with the criminal aura – Rogan.

It had been Rogan's sudden appearance that had set the warning bells clamoring in his brain. That could only mean trouble, for he and this man had reached the inevitable parting of the ways long before this, and both knew it. Rogan was smiling, cocky and amiable. He knew that didn't mean a thing.

Yet the strangest thing of all about this situation, with the whiff of the unreal about it, was that it hadn't fired up his thirst. Back when he'd thrown his bottle away he'd merely hoped he might be all through with the rotgut. Now he was certain. It might not be much but it sure was something.

'Get on with it,' he growled. 'You come by one pissant chunk of gold and suddenly it's the key to El Dorado. Is that your claim? And you say you're hard to hook, Damon? You're just another sucker.'

'No, not El Dorado, Steve. Not something fanciful. You see, Rogan and I had the assayer give us a cram course in local history. Of course, everyone knows Coronado scoured the South-west way back when looking for his cities of gold, but our man was able to tell us that ancient records prove a sizable party crossed the badlands south-west to north-east, allegedly fell foul of the Apaches or Comanches somewhere within sight of Spanish Mountain – named by the Spanish – and then just vanished, or so they say. This geezer did know they never got back to Coronado's base camp in New Mexico. But the most important thing of all that our friend revealed was the belief which originated back then and has been confirmed in a score of histories and official Mexican records of the great expedition since, that unlike the other search parities, Coronado's *hidalgo* captain, who never returned, was rumored to have actually discovered a city of gold. Never proved, of course, but I sure found it encouraging.'

'So?'

Walker appeared uninterested. It was just a pose. For while Damon was plainly highly excited about an ounce of gold and any amount of airy speculation, he had actually seen ... what he had seen. Seen it, felt it, suffered brutally because of it and eventually escaped with his life. The legend was no myth to him but bedrock reality.

'All right, history lesson over,' Damon said snappishly. 'You're going to tell me where you came by this arrowhead, Walker. I mean, *exactly*. Of course I'd have approached you openly with a proposition if you'd reacted normally to making such a find, you understand. But you didn't. You clammed up completely, even threatened Rogan if he spoke a word to anybody. This alerted me to the fact that you understood the significance of the find, and obviously had plans to get back here and track our trinket to its source yourself. So I had no option but to play my cards close to my chest, and when Rogan gave me the tip that you could be a soft touch for a sob story – if someone went about things the right way – why, I just put on my thinking cap.'

Walker understood. He glanced at the couple beside him.

'There's nobody croaking at Gun City, is there?'

'No,' Murphy blurted. 'They made us do it, Mr Walker. Honest. Like a fool I got in over my head at Damon's tables and he gave me the option of going to you with a cooked up sob-story, or going to jail. We're real sorry, honest.'

'Me too.'

Walker glanced up at Damon who now stood with Rogan at his shoulder. The pair made a formidable spectacle, big men with big guns and eyes like augers.

'You've wasted a lot of time and money,' he said flatly.

'I've been known to waste time but never money,' Damon retorted. He raised a well-shod boot to the log and rested an elbow on his thigh. 'Rogan tells me you've got a real bug in your bonnet against gold and mining and stuff ... what it does to places and people. I don't swallow any of that crap.'

'I happen to believe it.'

'Don't try and sell me that bill of goods. You're as greedy as the rest of us, mister. That's why I'm offering you a fair deal, Walker. Ten per cent cut of everything we find. And I just know we are going to find plenty. Nobody shoots away arrows with gold heads unless they have gold coming out their freaking ears.

That's what first got Rogan firing, then me. We know we're on to something big, as I explained just now, but I had to handle the deal this roundabout way because you're such a bonehead. But the gloves are off now, mister. I'll get to the source of this no matter what I've got to do. In short, you can make it real easy on yourself or as hard as it gets.'

There was no mistaking the threat in the man's words. But it didn't get him anywhere. Walker never buckled under pressure. Didn't know how. He'd made a decision once about that chunk of gold metal. It still stood. End of story. 'There's no gold,' he stated flatly, and Damon suddenly raised his boot and kicked him backwards off the deadfall.

The others had been waiting for this. It was their cue.

They swarmed in on him as he sprang erect. Rogan reached him first and swung a Colt barrel between Walker's upraised fists to to catch him hard across the temple. As he reeled, a fist sank into his kidneys and his legs were kicked away from under him, bringing him crashing to the ground on one shoulder.

Half-conscious, he was hauled half-way across the log and pinned there by the powerful hands of people who knew what they were about. Surrounded by remorseless faces, he blinked upwards to see Dutch Annie testing the point of her knife on the ball of her thumb. It was just a prick, yet a tiny crimson bubble of blood appeared instantly. The woman flicked her thumb towards him to spatter red blobs across his shirt front.

'Don't kill him,' warned Damon. 'You'll croak if he dies.'

'Don't tell granny how to suck eggs.' Dutch Annie smirked as she leaned downwards. 'Face first, big shot,' she taunted Walker. 'Seems to old Dutchie that you're one of them handsome dudes who thinks they're somethin' special. . . .'

Buckshot Sisk was pinning Walker's legs. He was strong but not strong enough. With a sudden explosion of sheer power, Steve twisted free of the man's grasp, then drove his right boot into the woman's unprotected face with every ounce of his strength.

It was a brute of a blow from a desperate man. Dutch Annie emitted a choked-off howl as she was flung backwards, clawing at her ruined face, blinded in one eye and choking on blood and smashed teeth as she fell like a coalsack.

A storm of blows and kicks rained down until Walker was seeing double and then triple. He tore an arm free and smashed it into a twisted face, felt the satisfying crunch of contact bolt up his arm into the shoulder muscle.

But the attack only intensified. Damon's party had been hired for this, had been waiting for it.

He took a stunning blow to the side of the head and found his face momentarily against the ground. He twisted desperately, knowing he was fighting for his life, knowing that Damon and Rogan were prepared to go all the way if they must. Gold fever. He'd seen it before. Worse than cholera.

He lashed out with his boot again but didn't know if it made contact or not. A second blow caught the side of his face and he was rolling in mud, barely conscious of Damon's shout: 'Don't kill him, just make him know who's calling the shots around here!'

He was bleeding. There was blood in his eyes and he didn't see Dutch Annie, with one eyeball hanging down her bloodied face and a gun in her fist as she ploughed headlong between Rogan and Sisk, and fired. The blast almost deafened Walker and the bullet drove into the earth beside his head with a hard smacking sound.

He heard the woman scream dementedly as she attempted to fire again at point-blank range. He caught the blur of movement from the corner of his eye. Damon. He was reaching towards the woman with his Colt extended at arm's length. The weapon exploded and Dutch Annie's ruined face seemed to implode as she dropped to both knees before toppling slowly forward, dead as anybody could be with a two-ounce chunk of lead in the brain.

'I warned you not to kill him, you stupid bitch!' Damon shouted.

'Stop this!' a dazed Steve Walker heard someone scream, and next moment a hysterical Connie Murphy threw herself across his body, trying to ward off his attackers.

'Murderers!' she screamed. 'You can't kill him, I won't let you.'

But this brutal game had gone too far. Buckshot Sisk daren't vent his fury over his paramour's death against Damon and Rogan, not with their threatening guns. But his rage had to find an outlet. Seizing Connie by the hair, he reefed her off Walker and backhanded her with all his force.

Walker thought he'd killed her.

'Cut it, you bastards!' he croaked, spitting crimson and fighting his way to one knee. Memories of another woman's violent death were suddenly overwhelming him. 'Let her be, she's done nothing!'

Sisk made to strike the girl again but Damon blocked his arm with his gunbarrel.

'What'd you say, Walker?' he panted, shoving the muzzle of his piece hard against her cheek, distorting her mouth. 'Don't hurt her?' he challenged. 'You don't give orders here, trail scout. This is my game and I call all the shots.'

He jammed the gun muzzle hard against the side of the woman's head. Walker cursed and tried to rise. A swinging gunbutt drove him back on to his side. Horrified, he watched Damon's finger tighten on the trigger. The pistol clicked but didn't fire.

'What do you know,' Damon taunted. 'Forgot the empty chamber under the hammer. But the rest are live – and you've served your purpose, blue-eyes!'

He made ready to shoot again. He might be bluffing. It was a risk Steve Walker couldn't take.

'Hold up, you miserable son of a bitch,' he shouted, at last finding the strength to come erect. He lunged drunkenly towards Damon, but suddenly someone was blocking his way. Rogan's grinning face swam before him. From somewhere deep down Steve summoned his reserves to swing a blow, a punch that carried all his remaining strength, desperation and fury in it. His knuckles exploded against Rogan's iron jaw and the big man went down as if pole-axed.

Staggering, reeling, Steve heard the gun cock again.

'No!' he gasped, holding up a hand. 'You've made your point, Damon. You're a miserable, dirty son of a bitch, but I'll play your game. Just leave these folks be.'

'Then talk, hardnose,' Damon barked, still with his weapon pointed at the woman. Walker began talking and he talked fast. He kept at it until a triumphant Damon eventually grinned in triumph and lowered his gun.

Five men peered down into the brush-choked hollow yawning at their feet. The one and only time Walker had ventured here had been in pitch-black darkness, and he and Cora Lee had stumbled down headlong here, almost knocking themselves senseless. But on emerging from the natural tunnel in the cliff astride a crater horse several violent minutes later, he'd veered away hard right where the slope was still steep yet navigable.

'Over there,' he said woodenly now, pointing, then led the way round.

'This doesn't look like nothing to me,' complained a battered Rogan. He rammed a gun muzzle hard into Walker's ribs, causing him to catch his breath. 'You couldn't be fool enough to try something tricky on me, Steve. Remember we worked together. I know you're a crafty son of a bitch, pal. But just remember. You signed me up for that job on account of nobody else had the brains or the balls for it. Well, I've still got 'em, in spades. I'm watching every breath you take, and you'll die six times before anyone else can even blink if you try a cross.'

Walker made no reply. He was saving himself, husbanding everything he had, staking everything on one slender hope based on what had befallen him the last time he had gone down that stone chamber leading into . . . what? He still wasn't sure.

Danger ahead and danger at his shoulder. Just like before. And again – all because of yellow gold.

Gold was an integral part of the lives of the strange people he'd encountered beyond the crater wall, a religion, their god, a way of life. They were consumed by something as dull and lifeless as yellow metal that you dug out of the dirt . . . as were those surrounding him now.

He glanced sideways at Rogan. Right up until that moment when Rogan had prized that arrow tip out of his saddle at Sentinel Rock, seemingly an age ago now, the man had been simply just another two-fisted, whang-and-leather tough outrider that the wasteland produced in numbers. But the smell of gold had metamorphosed him into someone capable of deceit and treachery, just as the mere evocation of Quivira had converted city-slicker Damon into a scheming killer. How could any sensible man not hate the stuff?

Achilles Cobb suddenly stumbled and almost pitched into the blackness to their right. Damon hauled the man back and Cobb cursed.

'Where's the freakin' sun?' he complained. 'Nothin's normal out here. There's been light for half an hour, the sky's clear, but no sun. Don't they say this mountain's haunted? I swear if I was back in Berbix right now you jokers wouldn't tempt me outta there if you promised me a naked Comanche squaw every mile. . . .'

His voice cut off abruptly. Quite suddenly, swelling in the sky in flaming colour, were the peaks of Spanish Mountain illuminated by the first rays of the still-hidden sun. The stars, which until now had continued to burn faintly in the Texas sky, had vanished, the glowing moon was reduced to no more than a sphere of white.

'An omen,' Damon panted breathlessly. 'A good one. And look! Now we can see down there – but I don't see any tunnel, Walker.'

'It's overgrown by that hanging brush,' Walker grunted. 'You can't see it until you're right on top of it.'

Damon jerked his chin at Buckshot Sisk, who went bounding down into the still deeply shadowed hollow, making for the far side. They could barely make out the man's figure as he called back:

'Somethin' here right enough, Mr Damon.' His voice began to echo as he disappeared. 'Uh huh, looks like a cave but it might be somethin' more.'

Damon clapped Walker on the shoulder.

'So, seems you were telling the truth after all. Glory, but I do admire a genuine high-minded hero. Only for me roughing up Connie I doubt if you'd have directed me to a good place to pee, let alone let me in on your secret. You've got integrity, Steve. You hate gold, make sacrifices to help good people—'

'You shouldn't have left those people back at the camp,' Walker cut in. 'This is dangerous country for anybody, let alone greenhorns.'

Damon waved dismissively.

'Let's stick to our knitting, hero,' he said, gazing down. 'So this is your route into your crater, as you call it. The place where you tangled with the men who killed your girl then shot gold-tipped arrows at you when you made a break.'

Walker just nodded as he led the way down the incline. He searched for sign his horse may have left but didn't find any. The earth here was unmarked. He didn't pause until he was standing in the tunnel-mouth alongside Sisk, with wide-eyed men gathered about him, staring into the blackness, excited, tense and scared.

He gestured. 'It's maybe fifty to sixty yards long. I don't know what's on the other side except that we worked our way in maybe half a mile into the crater before we were jumped by men we couldn't properly see.'

He was lying. In reality they'd been attacked almost the moment he and Cora Lee had emerged into the basin. He was banking everything on exactly the same thing happening again. He was unarmed, but at least knew what to expect here. The Quivira defence was impenetrable at this point. But forewarned was forearmed, he assured himself grimly. Maybe his knowledge of what they could expect when they emerged from the tunnel would prove enough of an advantage to save his life.

Maybe.

Rogan and Damon entered the tunnel and the latter struck a match. As walls and roof jumped into view they saw seepage, patches of pale limestone and leaf-litter. But that was about all. There was nothing to indicate the tunnel was in regular use. The faintest hint of light in the direction they were facing suggested that Walker's estimate of the length was accurate.

'All right,' Damon growled as the brief flame died, leaving them in semi-darkness. 'This is the moment we've all been waiting for and we'd better be ready for anything. Just remember, if we're to believe Walker there are dangerous men in here. But so far as we know, they don't have guns. We'll just have to believe that when we see it. We've come a long hard way looking for gold, and it's my experience that you've got to be ready to fight to the death for anything you want badly enough. Do you all want it that bad?'

Every head nodded. Damon had slaughtered one of their number less than an hour earlier, yet their cohesion remained unaffected. It was not loyalty or camaraderie that united such men but rather greed, and that could prove even stronger than blood-ties.

Another match flared, was held towards Steve's face.

Despite the battering he'd taken, the bruises, cuts and other marks of violence, the tattered shirt and the deep gash across his shoulder, he appeared balanced and fully composed.

The others only thought they might be about to confront deadly danger, but he knew it with bedrock certainty. Therefore he was calmly readying himself for the fight of his life. And how weird it was to be preparing for conflict against a virtually faceless foe who was plainly neither redskin, Comanchero, outlaw or any other breed of hellion known to the badlands. If he were to die he hoped it wouldn't be without at least knowing who had killed him. Or what.

'You're up, Steve,' Rogan said mockingly, eyes reflecting twin tiny flames of menace. He cocked his .45. 'This is your caper, but just remember—'

'Yeah, I know. No tricks.' Walker finished for him, starting off. 'All right, let's get it done with.'

Setting off, he forced them to hurry to keep up. He walked with a long easy stride with only the faintly strengthening glow from the basin end lighting the way. In back of him, Damon, Rogan, Sisk and Cobb were totally silent, hands locked around gun handles, footsteps muted on stone, wide-stretched eyes now taking in what could increasingly be seen of the landscape unfolding before them.

There were trees and brush clumps and glimpses of the high eastern walls now taking on the reflected hues of a rising sun that daubed them dun and grey. Near at hand, grassy earth rose steeply towards a sharp ridge. Off to the left was an abrupt drop.

Walker's throat constricted as he saw again the exact spot from which Cora Lee had plunged to her death as a result of a sword-stroke dealt by an armoured figure from out of the pages of half-forgotten history.

He forced himself to switch his attention now to the upslope to his right as he rapidly approached the mouth. His blurred recollection of this sector from which the unexpected assault had come, was of a row of cottonwoods and scattered boulders. Now, by daylight and with a quick eye, he also realized there were man-made barricades amongst the cottonwoods. He steeled himself for danger. It came as he strode clear of the tunnel and almost instantly heard a shout of alarm in an alien tongue coming from the trees.

The head and shoulders of a man appeared, helmeted and armoured. A gauntleted hand was swiftly drawing back the arrow nocked into the string of the heavy war bow.

But forewarned was indeed forearmed.

Steve Walker crouched low, then exploded into a headlong run as though shot from a giant's catapult.

Ignoring the angry shouts of Rogan and Damon, he dashed directly across the sward with long legs pumping and arms pistoning furiously, eating up distance. He covered some twenty paces at this explosive pace then hurled himself headlong into the long grass as someone screamed, 'To the right!' and bowstrings thrummed like a giant stroking a cello.

In an instant the sylvan scene was transformed into a roaring battlefield as someone fell choking with a feathered shaft through his neck, and rifles and sixguns opened up like a battery of cannon.

Suddenly, attacking figures came surging out of the cottonwoods, brandishing golden swords, their bodies protected by reinforced war shields of hickory and cowhide. Screaming.

Now Steve was up and running and making for the ridge.

Ten stretching paces, fifteen and he was still running.

He raised his eyes to the crest, fearing he might sight more helmeted figures swarming this way to deal with him, every instant expecting the thud of metal-tipped arrows in his back or the panther rush of booted feet behind.

Still nothing.

His anticipation and blinding speed were paying off. There had been merely some seven or eight warriors standing perimeter duty at the tunnel, all heavily alarmed and alert, when the party showed. But Walker's explosive rush to distance himself from his companions had caught the enemy unawares, and the moment the defenders concentrated their attention upon the main party and their storming guns, that battle had become all consuming.

Muzzle flashes flared between writhing bodies, and metal blades bit deep.

Shooting a wild look back over his shoulder as he neared the ridge crest a hundred yards distant, Walker saw Buckshot Sisk come stumbling out of the bloody mêlée, his right hand fumblingly groping for his left arm that wasn't there any longer. The hardcase fell to one knee, made it to his feet again and turned his shaggy head at the sound of a warning shout from Rogan as two fighters closed in on him. There was a hiss of blurring metal, the momentary glitter of sunlight on gold, then something hideous was rolling away across the slope pumping gouts of blood from ruptured arteries.

Sisk's severed head rolled to the very brink of the drop, then halted, bulging eyes staring back at its own body twitching in the grass.

Walker didn't see it all, just the head flying free.

Next moment he was over the ridge crest and tumbling down the far side, his senses absorbing fragments of sights and sounds. A horse trail winding away. A tower building several hundred yards distant with two men rushing from an arched doorway, shouting to one another in both Spanish and English. The glimpse of a city or town on the basin floor beneath a thin veil of morning smoke. The mountain. Then the arrow skimming over his head as he lunged to his feet, oaks and cottonwoods on his right screening off a massive rock slide.

He swerved and headed for the rocks.

Only one or two guns sounding now. If his party wasn't all dead back there they soon would be. He felt nothing. They were spoilers, no different from the renegades or Comancheros. They deserved to die. He hoped he deserved to live.

Shouts rose from both below and behind now. Somewhere there were hoofbeats. He was feeling every yard now, aware of every ounce of damage done to him at the campsite as the slope steepened towards the great boulders and slabs of talus ahead. Just a short distance to cover. If he could wriggle his long body in there someplace, find a niche to hide in, give himself half a chance to find out just who he was dealing with and how determined they might be to ferret him out. . . .

He almost made it.

Storming through the trees, he began clambering upslope with a vigour he was far from feeling. He was twenty feet up, then forty. He heard arrows striking well below, but the one that furrowed his shoulder caught him in mid leap and knocked him off balance.

He was falling.

He struck hard along his whole side, rolled downgrade over jagged-edged chunks of rock for a dozen yards before he was able to dig his heels into a crevice. There was shouting all about him as he swung his dusty head with the glare of the rising sun almost blinding him.

He started upwards again and steel fingers wrapped around his ankle. He kicked wildly.

'Kill the Comanchero devil!' a voice called in English. But another shout in Spanish countermanded the order. Now the enemy was upon him in numbers, clawing at him, dragging him down off the talus. His whole body tensed in anticipation of murderous blades in the instant before he felt the back of his head smash against stone, and the bright world to which he never expected to awaken turned black.

CHAPTER 6

CONQUISTADOR

Viceroy Juán de Contreras enjoyed leisurely beginnings to his days. Silent, barefoot servants and slaves brought in his hot drink and appetizers, his clothing was laid out awaiting his selection and the curtains overlooking the royal compound were silently and discreetly opened.

He saw that the day was clear following the overnight thunderstorm which had filled the crater with great booming echoes and raised the level of the river flowing beneath his windows. It was really only a creek but everything was upgraded and embellished here, up to and including Contreras' title. In the Homeland, viceroyships were bestowed, not inherited, yet there had been a viceroy overseeing tiny Quivira since the long-ago year when the Marooned Ones had made their last serious attempt to cross the hostile plains and find their way back to Santa Fe, to the Rio Bravo el Norte and, eventually,

Mexico. Contreras was forty years of age, tall, elegant and grave. He had worn the viceroy's robes for seven years following the record-breaking incumbency of his predecessor here, stretching back over fifty-two years.

His predecessor had been a very different man. He'd survived eighty-four summers in Quivira and had yearned for the Mexico he'd never known every single day.

Not so Juán de Contreras.

His father and uncle had perished at the hands of the vile Comancheros when he was but a child some time following the exiles' final failed attempt to make their way across the endless plains to the south. Contreras had grown up with little real conviction that Mexico or Spain existed anywhere but in the ancient books and scripts brought to this place by the Old Ones. His was the philosophical and reassuring belief that whatever lay beyond the battlement walls of the crater was hostile and evil while all that lay within was rich and good. And that it was his royal duty to preserve it and keep it so.

Despite this common-sense if limited attitude to his environment and its history, the man loved reading and talking about the old days. His bedchamber's entire south wall was covered by a mural depicting a coloured map which was a faithful copy of that drawn by an Italian cartographer drafted in the previous century. In subtle blues, muted yellows and with large areas of pale greens, the wilderness north of New Spain was laid out in considerable detail, with emphasis upon the fabled Seven Cities of Gold sought so ardently by the great Coronado and others and said to rival the breathtaking wealth of the Aztec Empire.

It was this map that had led the original settlers to the land now known as Quivira.

During Coronado's great quest he and his searchers from Mexico City had encountered countless bitter failures punctuated by the odd minor success further westward.

But this was an alien and savage land where Indians were a perennial menace, and as time and lack of significant success began to plague him, Coronado was compelled to spread his search nets wider in the increasingly desperate hope of finding his seven golden cities. Even a single genuine city of gold might have been acceptable at that late stage of the expedition.

The result of this decision had been the break-up of the main party into several individual groups of soldiers, geologists, map-makers and their slaves and attendants and the sending them off from base in different directions.

The largest party was given what was deemed the most dangerous destination, namely the vast and unmapped regions of north-west Texas that would ultimately become known as the Kree Badlands.

It was an expedition that might well have ended in total disaster but for the courage, leadership and wisdom of the man later to be known as the founder of Quivira, Captain Sandoval.

It was Sandoval who first realized the true scope of the dangers posed by the Comanches and Apaches, and who, having survived several murderous attacks on his columns, wisely refused to risk trying to fight his way back to Coronado but instead led his party into the stone heart of the badlands to seek refuge in the most remote and wildest region known as the Twisted Hills.

The Twisted Hills and Spanish Mountain region comprised some one hundred square miles of a geological nightmare-land, surrounded on all sides by the immense and empty plainslands. It was an island of rock centred in a sea of desert where, if the white man had ever ventured there, all traces of him seemed to have been erased, leaving it again as it had always been, part of the Red Empire.

It was said that even the eagle, coyote, buffalo, wolf or mountain lion could lose its way in this tumbling maze of shattered battlements, lofted towers, gashing canyons and criss-crossing dry creek-beds and towering cliff-faces rearing jaggedly into the pale skies. Sandoval's party promptly and shrewdly proceeded to 'lose' themselves in this bizarre land, created a home and their descendants had remained there ever since.

But the Mexicans attempted their first break-out after several months of safety and seclusion in their lost basin, which someone had romantically named 'Quivira'.

The party covered a hundred miles before encountering a war party of Apaches, resulting in a battle that cost them one tenth of their number and saw them forced to retreat to their basin.

The basin was self-sustaining with its own spring

creek running through it. Nature had hidden it away with the expertise of a conjurer; there were trees and deep caves for shelter, any amount of arable land, the only access by a natural tunnel running through the living rock. There the gold-seekers had established solid lodges and captured a number of Indian slaves, achieving a reasonable living-standard over a number of years before launching their next major break-out attempt.

This was planned down to the last detail. After weeks of preparation they patiently waited until one of the regular dust storms came howling across north-west Texas like the heavenly winds of Judgment Day, then they quit the refuge under cover of the duster and struck south-west.

They might well have made it but for one solitary drunken Apache dog soldier.

The buck was so drunk on tiswin he'd become separated from his hunting party heading south-east for their homeland in the Dragoon Mountains. He fell off his horse during the sandstorm, struck his ugly head on a boulder, came to twenty-four hours later and sat up to see immediately two things through blurred vision: his nag grazing in a hollow and an 'enemy army' advancing on horseback across the yellow plain.

When he realized the riders were not paleface traders, enemy tribesmen or pony soldiers but rather some strange breed armed and attired like nothing he'd ever seen, he panicked and took off at the gallop, barely pausing until he caught up with his war party a half-day later.

The raider chieftain was not intimidated by the buck's description of what he'd seen; decided that whatever it might be it was worth a second look through sober eyes.

The outcome of this chance encounter was the battle of Thunder Butte where the Mexicans were attacked by an Indian force that outnumbered them ten to one, a ferocious encounter that saw them forced to beat a strategic retreat. They undertook a deliberately roundabout route through the deserts to shake off their pursuers eventually before returning to their basin forty-eight hours later.

The council meeting that followed was the most important in the gold-seekers' history. The outcome was a unanimous communal agreement that escape was impossible, and that all future break-out plans be shelved and Quivira should become their permanent fortress home. There was much praying to God for assistance over the weeks that followed this momentous decision, and just a short time later a soldier digging for fishing-worms by the stream struck gold. An ancestor of the viceroy had been the leader at that time. He was recorded by the scribes as having declared memorably in a speech some time later:

'We are secure here. We could defend against an army, we have slaves and we have gold. What want we with Mexico? We have Quivira!'

These and other memories comforted the viceroy today as they did almost every day of his contented life.

'Hispana Nova,' he said softly, tracing his finger along the thin blue line representing the Rio

Grande. Then he moved his hand several inches above and to the right. 'Quivira,' he said, and smiled. He had long since come to believe that the outside world was all myth and supposition and secrets scrawled in the fading yellow pages of history. Only Quivira and its viceroy were real, as real as the majesty of Spanish Mountain.

An agitated aide thrust his head through a heavy curtain to remind his excellency that there were serious matters awaiting his attention; something so vitally important in fact as an attempted invasion of the sacred stronghold itself.

Contreras dismissed the man with a gesture. Of course the matter was serious. But his warriors had dealt with it with their customary efficiency. Of course he was both alarmed and curious about the bloody incident, but not so much so that he was prepared to hurry.

The girl duly arrived to help him dress.

She was young and slender, part-Spanish and part-Indian as were indeed almost all the inhabitants of the crater now. There had been but a dozen females with The Founder's ill-starred original command, with some twenty times that number of males. The proud Castilian blood-lines had thinned through intermingling with those of the Comanche slaves who inhabited the cliff city beyond the river. There was but a handful left who could trace their unsullied lineage all the way back to foundation, and those who could were as vain and arrogant as any pure-blood from Old Spain.

'It is a fine day, *Excelencia*.' The girl spoke in

English. Quivira was bilingual from Contreras down to the lowliest slave, reflecting the mixed-race composition of the original company which had set out upon the great journey of exploration from New Mexico all those years ago and never returned, to be eventually forgotten. 'The blue or the crimson, *señor*?'

He massaged his chin as he studied the garments laid out on the clothing-rack, then nodded.

'The crimson. More impressive when dealing with vermin.' He raised his brows. 'That's if any were taken alive, of course?'

'There may have been, I believe, *Excelencia*. I do know some were slain.'

'I would certainly hope so. My tunic first.'

The viceroy's days of dressing like a soldier were long behind him. No longer did he sport any armour other than a beautiful chased-gold breastplate which was worn over the tunic of silken cloth and beneath the hip-length cape of woven crimson. His boots were long and elegant and he sported a plumed headdress and golden wristlets, the completed ensemble a picture of grand affluence and authority which was set off by the way he walked from his chamber to be attended immediately by councillors and bodyguards, then made his way through a hallway of gold.

The palace of the governors was situated in the centre of the sizable compound which housed all the Spanish overlords. Indians and mixed breeds were restricted to the cliff city, the slaves confined to their riverside pens.

Set back from the river on the northern side of the

crater, which was some mile and a half wide at this point, stood the gantries, crushers and the long low ochre-walled stamp-mill of the mine where the slaves slogged in summer heat and winter cold in order to satisfy the Spaniards' insatiable love of gold.

And there was much gold to be found amongst this nightmare maze of the Twisted Hills standing before the imposing loftiness of Spanish Mountain. It was being mined by the primitive digger Indians long before Francisco Vasquez de Coronado accepted Viceroy Antonio de Mendoza's challenge to take himself into the Northlands beyond the Rio Grande and find, for the greater glory of Spain, the fabled Cibola.

There were said to be seven cities in Cibola, as the famed Fray Marcos had reported: 'Seven great cities, all under one mighty lord, each one greater than the last and all built of gold.'

The dominant irony of the great expeditions that had cost so many lives and ended with failure and bitter disappointment, was that the party under the command of Captain Vincente Romero was the only one of all the searchers actually to find gold in any quantity, yet in so doing he had been cut off from operational headquarters in New Mexico and had been eventually abandoned and left to his fate.

But the People were proud of what they had achieved, fiercely proud, and were always prepared to defend what they had made with the last drop of their blood. There was a visible grim reminder of some of the blood that had been spilled in recent times from the balcony where the viceroy paused to survey his basin today. Ornamenting four tall pikes above the main gate were the whitening skulls of men, ornamented with wide grey hats.

Comancheros.

The grey vermin were a constant danger out on the plains to the south but far less so here below the mountain where only the fiercest and most fearless of them ever dared venture, and then but rarely. Although relatively few in number, so warlike, well-trained and ferocious in battle had the Quivirans proved to be in defence of their hidden basin that no enemy had ever succeeded in breaching its outer perimeters or uncovering its actual location.

Until today.

At around daybreak while de Contreras dreamed in his big silk-canopied bed, someone had at last achieved the seemingly impossible and actually feasted their alien eyes upon the basin before the defences consumed them.

'Report, *Capitán*,' he ordered gravely, now fully ready to deal with this most serious of matters.

'Three intruders slain, two taken captive, *Excelencia*,' a soldier said.

'Comancheros?'

'Gringos, *señor*. They fought with valour.'

'Why were the two spared?'

'The accident in the mine last month, remember?' the captain reminded. 'We lost seven men, *señor*. The two Outsiders taken captive are both are tall and strong. I thought they should be spared the mercy of the quick death in exchange for life under the lash in the mine.'

A glacial smile worked de Contreras' features. From birth he had been taught to hate and fear all life beyond the basin. Outsiders had cost Quivira its freedom and, especially in the old days, had been responsible for the deaths of many Coronadans in their early escape attempts. Whenever an enemy fell into the Coronadans' hands, he could expect no mercy. Certainly they were in need of more slaves here, but the expression on de Contreras' face suggested strongly that he believed these prisoners should meet a swifter fate than the living hell of the mines.

'What brought them here, do we know, *Capitán*?' he enquired.

'What else but gold, *Excelencia*?'

'They came for gold, they shall have blood.'

'I understand, *señor* I shall make the preparations.'

'*Uno momento*,' de Contreras said as the man turned to leave. 'I am curious about these invaders. Where are these two being held?'

'They have been taken to the town prison.'

'Order my coach.'

'As you wish, *Excelencia*.'

Consciousness came by slow grey stages. It was almost comfortable at first, like waking from a deep sleep after a night at the bar. Then as light probed beneath the eyelids, the pain hit in the arm, the back, the shoulder – all over.

Walker groaned and rolled over to rest on his elbows. For a long moment there was light and shade and glimpses of grey walls. Then his vision cleared and he realized he was surrounded by a forest of legs.

He grunted in pain and in trying to shove himself off the tiled floor, discovered that his hands were chained together.

Something struck the back of his head and he actually felt himself grin. It was as though he was beyond pain now. Yet the blow seemed to clear his senses and he was seeing clearly enough as rough hands dragged him to his feet.

He blinked.

Standing before him were two large men wearing serapes fringed with gold thread. They carried spears. Above their helmeted heads, sunlight streamed through a high barred window and he realized he must be in a prison.

He turned his head away from those stony faces as a cultivated voice sounded behind.

'This is no Comanchero.'

Walker blinked.

The speaker was tall and fantastically attired in silk and gold. The face was handsome and cruel but also exotic, like a breed or race he'd never encountered before.

Flanking this imperious figure were more armed men who stared at him with dark-eyed hatred, half-filling the high-walled room from which a passage-way led off, presumably to cells.

He was alive and couldn't believe it. Yet he was in the hands of the enemy, so how come he was still breathing?

As though reading his thoughts the viceroy looked him up and down contemptuously, then spoke in that almost musical voice again.

'How did you filth find your way here? For longer than anyone remembers we have been secure in our isolation, now twice in a short time . . . vermin at the gates. Who are you and why did you come, gringo?'

Walker felt his fury ignite. These were the people who had killed Cora.

'I'm something you wouldn't understand,' he said distinctly. 'I'm a human being who doesn't murder innocent people – not some kind of freak show dandy in fancy—'

He was struck from behind. He staggered forward and attempted to head-butt the arrogant figure, who stepped back quickly. Another blow felled him to his knees again. The voice seemed to come from a great distance.

'My servant was right. Death is too good for such as these. A lifetime under the lash in the mine is far more fitting. See that they taste the lash first in order that they might fully understand what the future holds for them.'

Walker swept his boots around to slam forcefully into the man's legs. He heard him gasp in pain and shock before something smashed the back of his head and he knew no more.

For the second time in one day, Steve Walker found himself clawing his way out of a cocoon of unconsciousness; again awakened to find himself stretched out on a floor, but plainly not the tiles he'd seen before. This floor was stone-flagged and spattered with drops of blood. His blood.

He groaned and got to his knees, paused to shake his still ringing head, then somehow made it to his feet to stand swaying in the dingy half-light of the long adobe prison room.

'Judas Priest!' he gasped, clapping a hand to the back of his head. 'What hit me. . . ?'

'If it had been me you wouldn't be standing, walking or doing anything else ever again, you double-crossing son of a bitch!'

The voice was unmistakably Rogan's. It came from further along the shadowed room where Steve could barely make out the figure seated upon the floor with his back against the wall.

And he thought dully: Sure, Rogan would have survived. He always boasted he couldn't be killed. Maybe he was right.

He cleared his throat and spat blood. They'd removed his chains. By the look of these thick walls and a single tiny window high up, they didn't have to worry about anyone busting out of here. He moved about. It was difficult to guess the time of day because of the height and narrowness of the unglazed window.

'Where the hell are we?'

'In the local *calabozo*. Where else?'

'The others?'

'Dead, thanks to you.'

'Do you know that for sure?'

'All I know is that you expected those bastards to be waiting there by the tunnel. You led us into an ambush. You gave Americans up to . . . to damned savages!'

The man's contrived outrage almost brought a mirthless grin to Walker's lips. He did not see the point of reminding Rogan that it was he who'd set out on an odyssey of deceit and treachery against him, a man who'd done nothing other than treat him fair and square right down the line. But you didn't reason with men of this breed. He wished Rogan had not survived the clash at the tunnel. A golden blade through the guts would have been a fitting reward for his duplicity.

He turned his back, mustering up what he could recall of his flight, pursuit and quick capture. There was, he realized, no longer any uncertainty about the nature of the enemy here. That they were Mexicans or mixed bloods there could be no doubt. They certainly weren't ghosts or apparitions, but strong and vigorous men dressed in the apparel of another age. Some long-gone Spanish age, if he was to guess.

And reflecting on the man he'd spoken with, the obvious leader, he had to wonder yet again if the legends might not be true after all. He had no concept of the appearance of Coronado and his people, but their leader, de Contreras, certainly fitted in with his notion of what gold-hunters and dreamers of another age might look like.

He fingered the dried blood at the back of his head and gazed up at the dim light filtering through the window. Voices murmured from the passageway outside. From the distance drifted dim sounds of industry. It was like being dumped in an alien world where nothing made sense and the only certainty seemed to be that you wouldn't long survive.

BADLANDS IN MY BLOOD

After a time Rogan made several attempts at conversation, but drew no response. Slow and deadly anger was beginning to build in Walker's aching guts. Rage against this man, the betrayer who'd once almost been a friend. He fought against it, but this was no time or place for restraint. They were the captives of killers. They would surely be killed. What did he have to lose?

Steve Walker now regarded this man leaning his broad back against the grimed wall as every much of an enemy as were the Mexicans.

He approached the seated figure casually, but his pulsebeat was kicking hard. Rogan was idly toying with a straw. He glanced up with a mocking grin. He was battered and bruised with half his jerkin ripped away. He had a black eye and a tooth missing but still somehow managed to look more like a victor than the vanquished.

'What's on your mind, old pard?' he asked fatuously.

Walker kicked him in the face with all his strength.

Rogan exploded to his feet with a howl of animal wrath and swung a vicious blow. Walker ducked beneath it. His head snapped forward and found that hard jaw. Rogan was driven back into the wall but bounced back like a rubber man, a hooking fist crashing into the side of Walker's jaw, driving him half-way across the cell.

'C'mon, hero!' Rogan panted, beckoning with both hands. 'We got nothing to lose. These whoremasters are going to finish us anyway, so let's settle the big question we've been looking for the answer to ever since the day we met. Namely, who's the better man. Only thing, I've always known the answer.'

He lowered his head and charged. Walker braced himself and met the rush with a rigid shoulder driven in hard. The room seemed to shake with the force of the impact but Rogan didn't even flinch. The man was made of bloody iron!

Walker hooked viciously to the head and Rogan retaliated with a rip to the guts that had him hanging on. They wrestled, crashed to the floor, fought their way erect and continued battering one another with fists, boots, elbows, heads.

The racket carried and a key grated in a lock. The single heavy door swung open and the two big guards Walker had seen before came rushing in, swinging heavy staves.

'*Idiotas!*' one gasped. 'The gringo scum are about to be punished for their sins, yet they fight each other—'

'Stop them!'

The speaker was the third man to come striding in, a slim officer with a goatee beard, slapping his palm with a cane.

The guards rushed to obey and Walker and Rogan turned to confront them. But they had battered one another almost to a standstill by this, and proved no match for fresh and powerful men armed with weighty staves, which they wielded like experts.

Rogan went down first; Walker made certain of that. Next instant he took a stabbing thud to the forehead and went over backwards, striking the wall on the way down.

'Fifty lashes apiece,' the choleric officer bellowed. 'Take them away!'

A crowd comprising mostly Indians and slaves were on hand to watch the entertainment in the royal compound, and a small group dressed in ancient finery were highly visible as they watched from an overhanging balcony as first Walker then Rogan were thonged to whipping posts, where they duly received their prescribed punishment with the lash.

The leather bit deep into his back but Walker's jaws were locked shut; he didn't grimace and wouldn't. He felt a grudging pride when he saw that Rogan was handling his punishment in exactly the same way. The bastard was a man, no matter what his faults, and they were surely many and ugly.

Steve couldn't think of any of his many rugged acquaintances who could have taken this with such arrogant contempt.

When it was done the crowd chanted continuously for the viceroy until the man in out-dated finery whom Walker had confronted earlier leaned over the balcony with a tasselled baton in his hand.

'I have decided your fate, invaders!' he announced in a voice that carried. 'You will now escape the mine and instead be executed. Normally you would be immediately put to death and have your heads elevated on the spires of the gates, dogs of the plains. But in two days' time the Feast of the Saints falls due, and we shall offer your evil blood to the Divine Lord in holy sacrifice on that festival to help wash away our sins. As a special concession, as it was gold that brought you here, the royal executioner will sever your heads with a golden axe.'

The mob, some sixty to seventy in number, applauded wildly. They cheered, jeered and shook their fists while shouting: 'Comancheros!' even though it was plain they knew this was not the case. But 'Comanchero' was the ugliest insult in the Coronadans' lexicon.

Blocking his mind to the pain, Walker was scanning his surrounds with a scout's eye for detail. He noted the crater walls, the vast tangles of impenetrable thickets on three of the four sides, the tiers of ancient cliff dwellings built by the slaves, the flags of both Spain and Mexico fluttering at vantage points above hovel and palace alike.

It was all difficult to believe, but a man couldn't question the testimony of his own eyes. If he hadn't landed in a place like this it would have been impossible to imagine it. And as his gaze wandered up to the white cliff which concealed the tunnel, he felt only relief now that Cora Lee's end had been so swift and merciful. Had she survived she would have been condemned to life as a slave, or worse.

He studied the man who called himself the viceroy with hooded eyes. De Contreras' vanity and arrogance were almost laughable; he doubted the man could have been more full of himself if he was *El Presidente* of all Mexico. It seemed plain enough that Viceroy de Contreras enjoyed the spectacle of him and Rogan being punished and humiliated this way for the pleasure of the mob, before their heads got to ornament the compound gates.

Last of all he studied Rogan.

The flogger had really laid it into his Judas partner with his blacksnake, but Rogan had defiantly continued insulting, taunting and reviling the man even while absorbing the brutal punishment. Despite the fact that he'd taken enough to kill an ox, he still stood ramrod erect with blood flowing down his back, chin up, eyes fixed on infinity.

Again Walker felt that treacherous stir of admiration. He knew Joe Rogan would at least die like a man. He hoped they both might. It was something no man could ever be sure of until put to that final test.

A soldier in shimmering gold approached and brought the back of a gauntleted hand slashing across his face.

'My brother perished in the battle with you at the tunnel, *capón*. His *Excelencia* has placed me in charge of your execution. For every drop of blood my brother shed, you shall die a thousand deaths.'

He spat in his face and Walker looked at the sky. If you played the game you had to take the pain.

Deep-throated drums began to beat as the prisoners were marched from the walled yard through a series of archways back towards their prison. Men, women and shrieking children lined their route. They hurled missiles and insults and Rogan called them 'greaser sons of bitches', which naturally only inflamed them more.

Switching his attention to their tormentors, he knew now that they could only be descendants of those once engaged in the historic search for Cibola, difficult as it might be to comprehend. Yet these people were strong, if few in number, and the badlands were vastness itself. Such people could conceivably have survived here rather than attempt to cross hundreds of dangerous miles of enemy country to get back to where they'd come from, so he supposed.

But, of course, what did all that matter? All that really signified was that they'd invaded Quivira with evil intent and now would die for it.

This was what they'd promised.

But walking tall through all this howling and hatred, what Walker the plainsman was not doing, even now, was accepting this as inevitable. The thoughts running through his mind were those of a scout, Indian-fighter and traveller of the unknown lands who had learned, in a hundred desperate situations and across a thousand square miles of wilderness, that it was never over until it was over. No way would he give up hope until he was dead – as dead as those Comancheros grinning down at him from their white skulls atop the palace gates.

CHAPTER 7

CAME THE VERMIN

Rogan was singing softly and jingling his chains. Standing below the single high window, head cocked to one side, Walker listened to the sounds of the jailers, the street, the big mysterious night.

His back was giving him hell but that didn't even begin to diminish the energy surging through his battered body. Here, tonight, this plainsman was reduced to the primitive. He was an animal in captivity, a caged wolf. But even if every sense warned he was as good as dead, he still craved action, the chance to go out fighting, maybe take some of the enemy with him – anything but this.

The night had a strange atmosphere. Taut and explosive, as though something was about to happen. Would it be something that involved him? How could it? He'd seen game frozen square in the hunter's sights with better prospects than his own right now.

The singing stopped.

'You're doing it again, Walker.'

He stared. 'What?'

'Thinking too much. Seems you know a lot but you don't know it all. When you find yourself in a bad spot where there just ain't a solitary damn thing you can do, a smart man won't chew up energy and wear himself thin plotting and planning and kicking himself for slipping up. No sir. That is just plain dumb. What he does is just set quiet and easy and saving himself up so that when and if he gets a break or one itty bitty glimpse of a chance, why he's full of spunk and vinegar and might just have enough inside him to pull off the impossible. *Sabe?*'

'So, how come you're sweating and I'm not?'

Rogan's eyes flared yellow in the gloom. For despite his brag, he was sweating and couldn't deny it. He opened his mouth to speak but Walker abruptly held up a silencing hand.

'What?' Rogan hissed.

'We got a visitor.'

'Maybe the attorney-general's come to see how we're making out—'

'Shut up!'

As soon as they fell silent they picked up on the low murmur of voices from up front. Rogan cocked his head then sketched a woman's shape in the air before him. Walker nodded. It was a female voice all right, but soft and indistinct. They heard a door open and close, then their jailers' voices:

'A pie for the prisoners? She must be a fool.'

'A pretty fool, Virgil. Mmm, the smell is *bueno*. Your knife.'

'You are going to slice it for those pigs?'

'For us, Virgil, for— What is this?'

'Madonna! It is a dagger! Where is that harlot slave?'

The prisoners stood in wide-eyed silence for what seemed a long time before their reinforced door swung open and the senior jailer stood glaring at them with the light behind him. He was holding a long-bladed sticker and his face was livid.

'You have spies here!' he accused, brandishing the weapon. 'This I cannot believe. Who are they, or must I ask for permission to burn the truth out of you?'

'Could be my mother,' Rogan suggested wryly. 'Although . . . "harlot slave" did I hear you say?'

The door crashed shut and two deeply puzzled men stared at one another in silence. Someone, so it seemed, had actually attempted to help them escape. This was only slightly easier to believe than that pigs might fly.

The fleeing Damon realized he was galloping straight towards a line of livid gunflashes before he mastered his shock, made an instant decision and hurled himself headlong from the saddle.

The earth rushed up to meet him and he hit with a bone-jarring impact that belted the breath from his body and left him with just enough wits and strength to kick behind a deadfall. He lay huddled there while the night went loco crazy all about him.

They'd ridden headlong into the jaws of disaster!

Walker had led them to his secret tunnel as

promised; they'd followed him excitedly, armed to the teeth and ready for anything, almost tasting triumph before it happened.

Walker bolting.

The man's eyes glittered diamond-hard as in his mind's eye he pictured the scout's tall form racing away from the tunnel mouth and ducking low before vanishing into the trees on the right like quicksilver, heedless of his shout and Rogan's curses.

Next moment they were fighting for their very lives as figures dressed as he'd never seen before loomed up behind their sturdy barricades, longbows flashing in the early sunlight, golden-headed arrows thudding into Sisk and raking Damon's shoulder.

The beginning of a fight to the death, and a fight that maybe he alone had survived.

Walker had led them into that trap like blind mice!

He shook his head, too burdened by events even to hate or rage.

Slowly the images of the events he had been so vividly reliving began to fade and he was back in the present, absently massaging his hurting shoulder where he crouched in a deep crevice hidden in thick brush a bare half-mile from the battle zone.

With the queer detachment which can inhabit the minds of desperate people, the big man debated with himself the respective merits of continuing on west or cutting south. If he returned to the camp, he reasoned, there was no telling what hell he might walk into. The crater battle had raised a terrific racket that would carry many miles, could have been picked up by God only knew what ears. To turn south for Sentinel Rock, on the other hand, would be to admit complete defeat. The best he could hope for down there would be to find a loose horse, then strike back for civilization alone, something he doubted even Walker or Rogan would attempt.

And perhaps it would mean saying goodbye to the gold.

Damon's stare turned distant in the gloom.

In the hours he'd spent huddled still as death in this fissure high above the crater battleground where he'd managed to escape at the height of the battle, he had had nothing to do, waiting until night, but to study the strange place to which his quest for gold had brought him.

His hideaway commanded a partially obstructed view of the destination he'd come so far to find.

He'd had time to survey it all, the mine layout, the compound by the creek, the trudging slaves and their preening masters in their suits of velvet, their flowing serapes with gold trim. At first it had appeared like a fantasy created by a fevered brain. But as the day wore on reality sank in deep. He had even witnessed a public flogging attended by a crowd of a hundred or more including a florid glittering figure who was plainly *numero uno.*

If you were searching for touchstones of reality, then the whipping that Walker and Rogan had taken provided it, in spades.

Somehow it didn't surprise him to see that those two had come through it alive.

They were a rare breed. As was Chandler Damon, he had to add.

There'd been occasions in recent times when Damon feared the soft life might be slowly eroding what he believed had once been a man as formidable and heroic as a Rogan or a Walker. But the way he'd performed today – managing to fight his way clear in the heat of the battle eventually to make good his escape without the enemy even noticing his flight – that had been the action of a man who had lost nothing. He'd capped this by securing a hideaway which had stood him in good stead throughout the day. Obviously the enemy was not even aware they were one short in the number of captured and the dead. He'd found his hideaway and thus survived the searchers until dusk, when he'd been able to hustle away through the tunnel ahead of the arrival of the nightwatch in their golden armour.

He licked his lips.

That crater was a treasure-trove, a gold-seeker's dream.

And with that thought, he knew what he would do, what he must do.

He began to walk.

Stars were beginning to appear in a velvet sky as he caught his first glimpse of the campground clearing. The coach was still there but no sign of life. No fire, no sounds, nothing but the night. He hunkered down and waited. If all remained unchanged after an hour he would risk snaking down there and seeing what might be available in the way of water, chow, arms and ammunition. All he had right now was the rig he stood in and the belief that, if his nerve didn't fail and his luck held, he might still get to ride out of the badlands as rich as Croesus.

That hour took an eternity to pass.

Damon ghosted silently between the twisted trees, waited in shadows to check out the site at close range, then darted across the clearing for the coach.

'*Alto!*'

He froze in mid-stride. Even before he dared turn he realized the evening breeze was bringing him the sour, sweet scent of evil; a stink he'd not encountered – yet it was all too well remembered – since the last time plainsmen had brought in the carcass of a butchered Comanchero to be put on display in the Berbix square.

Scared? He was terrified. Yet the Damon who turned at last to watch the grey figures emerging from the brush clutching naked guns, was not a normal man prey to normal reactions. As he stared at the Comanchero party, knowing they could finish him any moment, he was still dominated by the gold, his great discovery, how he might still survive to make it his own.

This was optimism gone mad, yet quite the kind of madness that a Comanchero might recognize and understand better than most.

There were three of them. They had backtracked the Murphys, whom they'd sighted earlier in the day, riding a bay horse double in the far distance towards Gun City. Having spent the remainder of the day scouring the campsite and attempting to make sense of all the sign encountered, the trio had decided that whoever's camp and expensive gear this was, they would surely be back for it.

It didn't take long for a sweating Chandler Damon to figure out who was in charge. Two of the killers were regulation-looking ruffians, bristling with weaponry and showing broken and rotting teeth when they smirked at what must appear to them as a prize catch. The third was dark and tall, around forty years of age, with a hawk face still and watchful. A heavy black moustache curved over a thick brutal underlip, the eyes held the wolf gleam.

'I am Charro,' this one stated, the nickel-plated pistol in his kid-gloved hand angled casually at Damon's groin. A chill smile. 'I examine the documents in the coach. You must be the Señor Damon, no?'

Damon had never been more afraid. But as always he was capable of clear thinking in a crisis. He was dead six times over here if he didn't play his cards right. But what was the right way when you sat at the poker-table with players like this?

He took a gamble and replied honestly.

'Chandler Damon of Berbix. You've most likely heard of me.' He focused on the tall one, and added: 'Dealer, adventurer – gold-seeker.'

'Search him,' ordered Charro, his eyes not leaving Damon's. 'He will lie to us as surely as the moon rises soon, but perhaps his possessions may reveal why he dares venture here in our domain.'

They searched him but found nothing; they weren't supposed to. Times like this, Damon kept his cash in a secret sleeve inside his right boot. Plainly angered at finding nothing incriminating, the two searchers housed their pistols and drew long thin blades before looking to Charro for instruction.

It was a deeply held belief amongst towners and settlers on the frontier that Comancheros were something less than human, and Damon, confronting them at at close quarters live for the first time in his life, was ready to believe it.

Lean, snakelike, unbathed, dark of eye and oily of complexion, in grey garb, leathern vests and broad-brimmed hats, they appeared more like savage animals than men now as they quite plainly prepared to murder him.

The big man had never felt less ready to die, doubly so in light of the wonders he'd seen back east beyond the thicket wall. Up until now, with guns and stickers in his ribs and his knees knocking together, he'd had no option but to be a listener. Now, in this pregnant silence, he suddenly found his tongue again.

'Wait, wait, wait!' he pleaded, hands dancing expressively. 'Of course I have got money, bags of it. And it's yours if you still want it after I tell you about the gold.'

A knife-point pricked his throat and drew crimson.

'You lie as all enemy people lie,' the leader said with a sibilant hiss. 'There is no gold on the plains. The eagle knows this as does the rattlesnake. And so do we. Your money, pig. Show us or die!'

Damon was impressed by his own coolness as he raised his right leg and felt for the stitched-in boot purse. In truth, now that they had allowed him to live this long, affording him time to recover from his shock and get his brain gears meshing, he was feeling almost optimistic. The talk, the con, the persuasion and the convincing – these were the things he handled best of all, his tools of trade.

Calmly he produced his fat billfold and proffered it to the two with the blades. But it was Charro who plucked it from his fingers and snapped it open. Despite himself, the Comanchero's eyes popped wide at sight of the wad of big bills.

'*Madre de Dios!*'

'How much?'

'Chicken feed.' Damon rested hands on hips and struck a confidently casual pose, as hard a thing as he'd ever called upon himself to do. He was looking and sounding like a winner once more as he again focused on Charro.

'I found me a city of gold. Coronado's city, although I doubt that'd mean anything to you. Not five miles from right here where we're sitting.' His eyes burned with genuine excitement now. There was no need to fake on this topic. 'Why do you think I'm here? I'm the richest man in Berbix, as that billfold proves, and I've lost count of the men I've seen ride into the wasteland and never return.'

He paused to fling both arms wide.

'Just look at me. Ask yourselves what other reason would a big-dollar rooster like me have to be found out here all alone one starry night a hundred miles from home, no guns, no drinking-water and not a lousy friend, bodyguard or guide in sight, for God's sake? Come on, Charro, you look like a reasonably smart *hombre*. You put forward one reason – any reason other than gold – that would explain what you are seeing with your own eyes. If you honestly can, then that's it. Go right ahead and cut my throat.'

He waited. Seconds dragged by. He knew his situation was still desperate. Yet as he'd talked, he'd felt the tension ease and the balance subtly shift. The grey vermin looked every bit as lethal as before, and their wicked blades still reflected the cold starlight. But there was a change, and they were surely listening intently to his every word. Always a gifted liar, Damon at this point had the added advantage of speaking the truth. There was gold, and he was proclaiming the fact, not a lie. His face glowed with sincerity and his body shook with emotion. He was a tub-thumping holy-roller selling the sinner on Jesus – or the Comanchero on the thing that dreams were made of. He was in full oratorical flight.

'You see, boys, I heard a whisper about something out here,' he continued confidentially. 'Not something just big – huge. A man came to me with a piece of gold that convinced me he'd stumbled on to Quivira – and the son of a bitch was right! We are sitting on it, *amigos*, and as your prisoner and your new best friend, I'm inviting you to put those cutters away, give me a little something to ease my dry throat, and I will lay something before you the like of which you hard-luckers couldn't even begin to dream of.'

A half-minute that seemed as long as an hour was to pass before he would discover whether his silver tongue could work its magic on subhuman trash as it did with real people.

Until at last Charro grunted and thrust his gleaming revolver into the red sash of his waistband, and said: 'If you lie you will take eternity to die.'

Damon began breathing again.

Charro grunted an order and an ape posing as a man promptly produced a flask of evil-tasting black liquor and thrust it at him. Damon's hand shook as he took it. The trio assumed more comfortable listening positions, waiting. Damon never prayed but something akin to a prayer of thanks slipped silently past his lips as he took a powerful swig, waited a long moment until able to breathe easy, then began again.

The longer he spoke the better he sounded even to his own ears. He talked until they truly believed, and by the time he was all talked out he was no longer just one desperate gold-greedy man all alone in enemy hands. He now had friends. What was more, his new friends had other friends not all that far away with whom they could communicate via the heliograph, now the moon had risen. Brave fighting men with guns and ammunition, so he was assured. Men who lived their whole lives dreaming of wealth and gold, which was like saying they were his brothers.

Damon felt no shame as a tear of pure relief and excitement coursed down his cheek.

'*Amigos, compadres,* this is the greatest day of all our lives!'

He knew he was overplaying his hand now. So did they.

'Talk, do not babble like a woman,' Charro growled as his men went to fetch their horses. 'How far?'

'Only a few miles. But there's no way you'd ever find it if you didn't know the way. Not through the thornbrush. That's why those Mexes have been able to live here God knows how long. It's the kind of hideaway only desperate men could ever have found, so I figure, and I guess they've been smart enough to stick to their own patch and not venture outside too often.' He paused to grin. 'But you jokers are looking at the man who'd find gold if it was stashed in the devil's skivvies.'

Charro seemed to be thinking out loud as he said:

'For as long as I can remember there have been stories of strange men hiding out here somewhere, and indeed several times they have been killed by us and their gold and weapons brought back to the Palo Duro where we also live where none can ever find us.'

He paused to nod at Damon.

'You see, this is the main reason I believe your tale, townsman. The gold and the strange ones – they link with what we already know.'

Damon was suddenly all brisk business, sure of them now.

'How many men can you muster all-up?'

'As many as eight or ten, perhaps.'

'All armed as good as you geezers?'

'We never travel the great plains any other way.'

Damon promptly hunkered down, a picture of concentration as he began to talk and scrawl in the dirt between his boots with a stick. The fact that he was throwing in his lot with the scum of the southwest did not even enter his thinking, much less disturb him. In the space of one day he had descended from Mr Big running his own show to a hunted animal teetering on the brink of death as a Comanchero prisoner, but now had clawed his way back to playing Mr Big again. Why should he give one sweet damn about his methods, providing they paid off. He would first get the gold, then worry about Charro and co. He'd suckered them in; no reason he couldn't sucker them out.

'This tunnel is the only way in and out of the basin,' he confided, pointing with his stick. 'Ten of us packing shooters, who know what to expect, stacked up against spicks with swords who we'll take by surprise. It'll be almost a shame to take the money. But to improve our attack, we'll need a diversion. You know, something to distract them. You following me, *compañero*?'

'Keep talking, Señor Damon. You seem to know what you are speaking of.'

'Ain't that the truth.'

Steve Walker stood below the prison window. The light was fading fast. Unless they could count on an earthquake or a miracle, this would be the last sundown.

The heat of the day was fading and he'd heard their two night sentries driving off the youths and young children who'd had a fine day of it standing outside the prison screaming taunts and insults at the hated 'Outsiders'.

His stomach grumbled as the faint waft of cooking meat hit his nostrils. They had not been fed. They would die upon an altar beneath a crucifix upon the palace square, so a day-jailer had been happy to inform them. Blood sacrifices. Apparently the religion here was an odd mix of Christianity and Aztec paganism; the God of love and the gods of blood.

He heard Rogan cough as he lighted a cigarette. Walker couldn't understand why their captors had left them their tobacco. Thirst and starvation could knock a man around physically, but as long as he had a smoke his spirits were inclined to hold up.

As he tugged out tobacco and papers, he called:

'Hey, Pedro! What happens to Outsiders when they die here? Do you bury them?'

'Bury Outsiders?' a voice responded. 'We feed them to the buzzards, of course.' Walker lit his cigarette and drew deeply.

'See where your curiosity gets you, Walker?' growled Rogan. 'You'd be better off believing they might have buried her, wouldn't you?'

Rogan understood him too well, knew Cora Lee had been preying on his mind ever since their capture. A man in chains waiting for death tended to think about loved ones, and how he might change things if he had his time over.

Of course he could not blame himself for events the night Cora Lee and Stan Chip died, he knew. They'd fled blindly through the thornbrush and literally stumbled upon the secret tunnel that had led Cora Lee to her death. Even so, her spirit was strong here, and for some reason he could not explain it seemed harder to accept the reality of her death in this place than it had been in Sulphurville.

He knew now that it was some psychic need to return to the region where he'd lost her that had played a major role in his decision to bring Damon and the Murphys out to Gun City.

'Dog got your tongue, Walker?'

'What's your trouble, Rogan? Need to jawbone to keep you from fretting about tomorrow?'

Rogan was more his enemy than Damon, the hardcases, even the Comancheros. For he had been a trail partner. They had ridden the river together before gold had corrupted Rogan and exposed the wolf-dog in him. He saw him now as a Judas, and a plainsman didn't have a lower designation than that.

'You know I don't scare, Walker.'

'Every man's scared of something.'

'Maybe.' Rogan's tone told him that he really did want to talk. 'In fact you're right. Know what scares me? The one thing?'

'Honesty?'

'No, I'm serious.'

'So am I.'

'Buzzards.'

'What?'

'That's right. Loco, ain't it? I mean, a buzzard's no worry to a man until he's dead.'

'Well, this time tomorrow they'll most likely be worrying you then, won't they?'

'You're really something you know, Stevie boy,' Rogan sneered. 'Always got to stand a little taller than the next guy, don't you? Or try. But you are nothing special even if you think you are. Think on it a minute. Only for you and your high-and-mighty ways we wouldn't be here, and those others wouldn't be dead. It's all on your plate, pilgrim, every ounce of it.'

Walker let smoke trickle from his nostrils, the dimming light sheening his thick hair.

'How do you figure that?' he wanted to know, aware that he also needed to talk.

Rogan gestured impatiently as he paced to and fro on the end of his chain.

'The whole damn thing about the gold, of course. You and me stumbled on to that little gold arrowhead which we both realized was something real big. But instead of reacting like a normal man, all you wanted to do was get it off of me and throw it away or bury it – make out it never happened. So instead of you and me sitting down to plan out what it all meant, and mebbe how to make ourselves rich if it meant what we hoped, I had to go look up Damon. And that's where things started going wrong. You want to try and deny that?'

'No.'

'So you admit it was all your fault?'

'No way. Yours, mister, all yours.'

'How do you figure?'

Walker's cigarette was almost smoked out. He conserved it for one last draw.

'You thought I was cracked because I wanted nothing to do with that gold. Any gold. You knew I'd always been that way but you thought it was a pose, all talk. You figured that, given the chance, I'd reach out with both hands for any gold that came my way. But I didn't, mister, and I was right.'

'Right?' Rogan gesticulated. 'Corpses all over, you and me waiting to be carved up like Thanksgiving turkeys tomorrow, all because of what you done. And yet you still claim you were right?'

'I know what gold does. I've always known. That's why I'd never guide a prospector anyplace out here. I want this piece of Texas to stay the way it is, not suddenly crawling with greedy bastards like you ready to lie and cheat and murder just to get rich. And when I say I was right – take a look at what that piddling arrowhead's done ... just a couple of ounces of the stuff. All those people dead because of it and not one of them a dime better off. And every man Jack would be alive tonight if you hadn't taken that piece to Damon. Deny that, Judas!'

'You'll call me that once too often, damn you!'

'Or what, Rogan? What will you do? Too bad we can't have it out. If I die I'd as soon go knowing I'd taken you out first.'

'You and how many others?'

'I'd have to be a better man than you on account you are no man at all.'

Rogan cursed him but Walker did not respond. He was angry but knew anger was a foolish waste of strength. And even though he meant every word he'd just spoken, he knew it was the tension and the fate hanging over their heads that was reducing them to squawling like trapped animals.

Time passed on leaden feet.

He must have dozed, for he was suddenly aware of voices outside. Gazing up at the window he realized it was night.

'And what is this you bring me, slave girl?' He recognized the sentry's heavy accent. 'Malt whiskey or pulque?'

A woman's voice answered, 'Whiskey. For you both. I feared you might be cold.' The conversations and sounds of movement continued for some time as Walker stood rubbing the side of his head and frowning hard. He knew the slaves roamed at will; there was no escape from Quivira for them. It was the woman's voice that engaged his attention, for he thought it sounded disturbingly familiar somehow.

He glanced in Rogan's direction. He was likewise listening intently. Rogan spoke quietly:

'What's going on, do you figure?'

'Seems plain enough. They're having a drink.'

'On guard duty?'

'We're thinking like Americans. Maybe things were different back in Coronado's day for the soldiers.'

Momentarily the prisoners were reminded afresh of the true strangeness of their situation, aware of the enormous sweep of time which separated their captors from the Texas of the 1860s.

But there was one constant between one century and another; you still slew your enemies.

It was quiet for some time after this. Indeed the silence prevailed for so long that the prisoners found themselves staring quizzically at one another through the gloom, wondering why there were now no voices, no shuffle of pacing feet to be heard, nothing at all.

The abrupt sound of a key grating in the lock

came loud as a gunshot. The two stared fixedly as the door began slowly to ease open.

'Let me guess,' Rogan shouted defiantly. 'You're going to kill us tonight?'

No response came from the dim figure stepping inside. Walker clenched his fists and moved back until he had the wall behind him. He would make one last fight of it.

Then: 'Steve?'

He stiffened. His heart clenched painfully in his chest as the slender figure drew closer.

'Steve. . . ? It's me.'

My God! he thought. He was going crazy. It could not be!

But it was. With a cry the woman rushed to him and there was just enough light to make out the pale face and wide blue eyes of Cora Lee.

CHAPTER 8

DEAL WITH THE DEVIL

De Contreras sat drinking sweet red wine from golden goblets with his captains. From the walls of the council chamber portraits of former viceroys stared down upon the man now responsible for the destiny of Quivira. Some subjects were already aged when they sat for their portraits, others were youthful and black-bearded with the look of aristocrats and warriors. De Contreras had already been painted, but the picture would not be hung before his death, as was the custom – and tonight His Excellency was much concerned with how he might be remembered by those who came after him.

Thus far, his reputation and status were rock-solid. A scholar and athlete as a youth, de Contreras had risen swiftly through the ranks as an administrator and planner. But the talent for which he became best known, and which eventually led to him being installed as viceroy, was that of a hunter and killer of Comancheros, the Enemy People of the Quivira.

Over their long decades of isolation and independence there had been many dangers for the people of the basin, but none greater than that posed by the Comancheros: those who deal with the Comanches.

Originally it had been the Indians who'd thwarted all hope of escape from their exile, but in time as the Comancheros grew stronger, raiding, plundering and murdering across north-west Texas and beyond, the Indians were relegated to the position of mere henchmen and suppliers to the grey killers whom Quivira knew as the Enemy People.

From Comanchero prisoners whom they had taken, and subsequently put to the torture before slaughtering them in the most gruesome ways imagination could devise, they'd learned that the vermin had long known of their existence in the Twisted Hills. But due to the Quivirans' security, ability in battle and the ferocious manner in which they dealt with any enemy who came too close, whether by accident or design, they had never had the stomach or the necessity to warrant staging a serious search for those who shared the wilderness with them.

From time to time and for various reasons, the Spanish fighting men would leave the crater and go hunting Comancheros as one would coyotes or wolves, a skill they had developed into a science over the years. As a consequence of this ferocity the Comancheros had never got to discover the secret brush-choked entrance to the basin, as Texans had recently done.

In his pre-viceroy days, the then Captain de Contreras had been the most successful of these Comanchero-hunters and was generally credited with being responsible for keeping the common enemy at bay for so long.

But the reason he had called a council with his captains tonight was to discuss the latest threat to their security, only the second non-Comanchero threat on record.

'Twice they have invaded in mere weeks,' he declared soberly. 'Of course the enemy scouts will perish tomorrow. But I believe there is reason to believe that not all the invaders were slain or captured in the battle. Might this not be so, Capitan Chavez?'

A smartly presented man with black goatee and an ancient blade-scar down one cheek, nodded emphatically. 'There was another, Excellency. Tall, dark of complexion, the leader we suspect. In the heat of the battle he was heard to be called "Damon" or some such name. Afterwards we believed he may have been wounded and crawled away to die, but the searchers have not located him. I would like to seek permission to extend a search beyond the basin, *señor.*'

With sudden energy, de Contreras rose and strode to a window overlooking his tiny kingdom. He was proud of the way the People had survived and prospered here and felt the weight of his responsibilities keenly. Gazing upwards to the south-west extremity of the basin, the vulnerable corner which was guarded day and night by heavily armed sentries, he was torn as he always was between caution and necessity.

If, as the viceroy suspected, a survivor of the battle might have escaped, then this posed an immense and immediate threat to the basin. If word of their riches ever reached the greed-driven outside world, Quivira would surely be doomed.

Yet the risk of sending searchers out now, not knowing if it were safe or whether perhaps there might be strong forces simply waiting for him to make such a move, in the end proved the stronger concern.

He turned back to the room.

'The gods have protected us thus far,' he said. 'We are the holy city and our enemies are venal and weak.' He gestured at the sombre faces of his antecedents watching from the walls. 'The history of our forefathers tells us they were strong and united of purpose, but at times of peril or uncertainty they invariably chose to remain behind our high walls rather than venture into the accursed Outside. So shall we be strong and confident that our secret will not be spread abroad by that escaped man who I believe will not survive, or by anyone else. Of course, all soldiers will remain on full alert until we are certain all is well. Now, be of good cheer and fill your goblets again that we may drink to the gods to whom we shall offer up the blood of our captives when the sun is risen.' He thrust his goblet high and shouted: 'I give you Quivira!'

'Quivira!' a dozen hearty voices responded. And the faces of the dead leaders seemed to smile upon them, but whether in admiration or pity there was no telling.

'About time you got here,' Chandler Damon snapped truculently, and wondered just where he found the nerve. For confronting as frightening a sight as any plainsman could conceive of in this slowly strengthening moonlight, his heart was pounding and there was a cold colic in his bowels. Damon was so scared he wanted to throw up, but instead clamped his jaw muscles tight and made an imperious gesture.

'What the devil kept you, damnit?'

They stared at him speculatively, a dozen Comancheros encircling him in silence. Charro's men had proved as good as their word, bringing in three other squads from various points of the compass with the assistance of signals transmitted by means of mirrors and moonlight, the desert heliograph.

Mathematically, it tallied that if Damon was afraid of three of them, then a dozen would scare him four times worse. Prior to this encounter, he'd been taking great pride in the way he was handling himself out here on the savage frontier, so far from the natural surroundings of his plush office, his bodyguards and his adoring women back in Berbix. This was blood-and-guts reality, just like the old days, and despite ten years of cushy living it charged him up to realize he could still cut the mustard as in his younger days riding the owlhoot.

But the presence of Comancheros in numbers had

punctured his confidence and brought him to ground. A bunch of Comanches this size would scare Old Nick himself. Standing in this primitive setting encircled by brutes who made paint-daubed Comanches or Cheyennes look like the local church choir by comparison, he was frozen with fear and wondered if he might be due for a heart attack.

Yet he somehow survived and reminded himself that he had always been a good gambler, and that this gambler must rely upon bluff – would play it straight and hard right down to the wire because he'd always been a natural actor, as any successful con man and crook must be.

'Cat got their tongues?' he snapped at Charro.

To his immense relief, the tall killer actually grinned, evil black moustache stirring, snaggled teeth glittering like a hound-dog's.

'The man has the tongue of a fool,' Charro explained to his skulking henchmen. 'But he also speaks of gold, *compañeros*. I think you should listen to him.'

The ruffians fiddled with their guns and studded knife-handles which jutted from ornate belts. Their scarred and pock-marked poker faces looked away from the captive and turned instead to the Old One.

He was sparse of hair and very rotund with a broad fat face ornamented by immense grey moustachios which thrust out on either side like the horns of a bull. His name was Walloon, as Damon was to discover, and that he was a leader of some description was patently apparent. With a surprisingly light step the Comanchero approached the big man and stared ferociously into his face; he smelt like curing skunkhide.

'Walloon has never known a Texan who did not lie,' he wheezed and hissed. Then he shrugged and dropped the scowl. 'But Charro has the brain, and if he believes, then Walloon shall listen. So speak while you still have a tongue, *señor*. Speak fast.'

It took something like ten minutes for a sweating Chan Damon to convince his extended audience – Walloon in particular – that he had indeed stumbled on to something momentous and lived to tell about it. As reward for his articulateness he was granted further time to describe the basin and its defences in detail, then to go on to outline his proposed plan of attack.

No longer so fearful that his flamboyant life might be brought to an abrupt conclusion at any moment, Damon went on speaking freely and lucidly, accompanying his ideas with sketches in the dirt drawn with a twig as moonlight began to wash the clearing.

Naturally he put the best possible slant on what he was proposing, while at the same time making sure his audience knew that they would be up against heavy odds and might well all perish despite their superior weaponry should they give his attack plan anything less than their total commitment.

Meanwhile, as always, Damon was thinking feverishly about Damon. Here he was, whipping up enthusiasm for an assault upon a whole tribe of Mexicans and Mex-Indians who were armed, well-trained and committed, while his 'strike force' comprised a handful of scum who would sooner cut his throat ear to ear than drink malt whiskey.

If they lost, he would have nothing to worry about. He'd be dead. But should they triumph and get their hands on Coronado's gold, how long might Chandler Damon expect to survive the victory? He would be of no further use to these fetid henchmen, and they were men who killed for fun and entertainment.

As he saw it he had no alternative. Escape was impossible. His new 'friends' wouldn't allow him to get ten feet. But the second factor was even stronger. Damon had actually seen the gold of the weapons, the armour and the ornaments with his own greedy eyes. It had been a sight to make weak men strong, a coward brave. He had to believe both in victory and his oft-proven ability to survive and prosper no matter who else went under.

'So, what do you say?' He was challenging them again now, a cigar in one hand, strolling up and down impatiently looking every inch a leader of men. 'If you don't believe my story I can direct you to the tunnel and you can ride in and get yourselves slaughtered for nothing. If you do believe, let's rehearse our battle plan, and by first light we could be the richest men in the state of Texas.'

They hated him, mistrusted him, would fight amongst themselves for the privilege of disembowelling this arrogant interloper who treated them like underlings – under different circumstances. Yet Damon was never safer. He was a born salesman and was never more eloquent. They believed – wanted to believe. They could smell the yellow gold now, and

Damon at last stopped leaking cold sweat when old Walloon hauled an ivory-handled sixgun from the broad belt holding up his paunch and passed it to him.

As of that moment, they were now *compadres*.

CHAPTER 9

BACK FROM THE GRAVE

Cora Lee rolled up her sleeve to reveal the long livid scar which ran the entire length of her slender right arm.

'That was where the sword caught me, darling – I can understand your thinking I'd been killed.'

'But I saw you go over that cliff. . . .'

'I struck a ledge about ten feet below the rim. I lost consciousness, was amazed when I came to in the slave quarters below the cliff city. I was certain they would have killed me. They told me they would have done so had I been a man. But they need women for slaves and . . . and for breeding. Oh, Steve!'

She threw both arms around him and held him fiercely to her. Stunned and speechless for the moment, Walker stared over her crown of dusty auburn hair to see Rogan twitching with eager excitement as he strained towards them, extending his leg chain to its limit.

'For Pete's sake will you give up on the rainbows and moonshine for a minute?' the man hissed. 'Tell us what's going on out there, girl. How'd you get in? How long have we got to—'

'I drugged them,' Cora Lee told Walker, now holding him at arm's length. 'Slaves have the run of the place in the kitchens and I know where they keep their medications, including the opium and sleeping-potions for the *hidalgos*.' She motioned at the entranceway. 'I brought them hot coffee and flirted with them while they drank it. All of it. They will be lucky to wake up by morning.'

He kept touching her. He couldn't help it. Although dressed in rags and burned brown by long hours in the outdoors, Cora Lee looked amazingly different yet achingly the same. Steve Walker might still be knocking on death's back door in this place, yet it felt more like he was in heaven. For this woman's apparent loss had been the worst blow he'd ever suffered, had affected him so deeply over time that he had become almost a stranger to himself.

'I shake to think what might have happened to you if I hadn't let Damon con me into coming out here again the way he did, honey,' he confessed, his breath catching in his throat. 'I was so damn sure you were gone that I never wanted see Spanish Mountain again—'

She cut him off, her finger pressed against his lips.

'I understand, darling. But of course I never even

dared hope you might ever come searching for me, as I knew you'd have had to believe I'd been killed in that fall,' she said.

She darted a glance at Rogan, who was quivering in expectation, eager as a racehorse at the starter's gate.

'But we must hurry now before the jailers are discovered. I want you to put their tunics on over your clothes, don't wear your hats. If we're lucky we might be able to cross the creek lower down then work our way towards the south-west wall and the tunnel, although God alone knows how we'll get past the sentries there. . . .'

'Why don't you leave us to fret about that, Cora girl,' Rogan said eagerly. 'On account you're looking at about the meanest two-man team in all Texas. Keerect, Steve?'

What Walker was looking at was a double-dealing Judas Iscariot son of a bitch. But Rogan was still the toughest man he'd ever known, the very best ally a man could have at his side when assessing what might lie ahead here.

'Does that key undo our leg chains?' he asked the girl.

Within moments they were free, with Cora leading the way for the door. In the adjacent room, one jailer lay with his back against the adobe and his sorry head resting on his chest. The other was close by, face down, out to the world.

'One we sure owe you, honey,' Rogan whispered as he went lunging out.

It took but a minute to strip the unconscious men

of their rigs and put them on.

'Always knew I'd look cute in a dress,' Rogan quipped, high on exhilaration and brimful of confidence. He snatched up a gold-handled halberd some six feet long, and immediately looked far more lethal than cute. He watched Walker slip a foot-long dagger into his belt, then fit a helmet to his head. He nodded approvingly.

'I've been thinking fast, Steve. And Cora's right. The way this place is laid out, the tunnel's our only hope. And thinking on the way they've got those barricades set up in the trees facing the tunnel, I reckon we should stand at least an even money chance of getting above them and taking them from behind and . . . Judas!'

'What?' Steve rapped.

'Just thought. What if they've got our guns now? Cora, do you know if they—?'

'It doesn't matter a damn if they do or don't.' Walker cut him off. 'But I agree with what you say. It's the tunnel or nothing, and every minute we waste here could be the minute that makes the difference. Cora, you show us the way.'

Slim, trim and so light on her feet, the girl quickly had the two men stretching their legs as they sped away from the prison across a wide grassed slope, making for a cluster of buildings lower down. As he ran, the tunic flapping round his legs and the wicked halberd shimmering in the moonlight, Walker looked up the rise past the heroic statues and ornamental columns, beyond the walled courtyards where they were scheduled to be executed, to the loft of the viceroy's palace. A fleeting moment of unreality possessed him as they rushed on; Steve Walker, Texan plains guide of the 1860s, running for his very life by moonlight through a Spanish city straight out of another century. But it was all very real.

As real as a public flogging, a beheading in the square or a halberd through the guts; as real as that heady smell of freedom and the blood surging through the veins with every heartbeat urged him to live.

The buildings loomed. Cora Lee led them to the mouth of a paved arcade at the far end of which they sighted moving figures. They waited. The figures disappeared.

'It's the only way,' she hissed. 'I think they were just citizens on their way home from the wine tavern.'

Could have been, but weren't.

As the running trio approached the far end of the hundred-yard-long arcade, the two captains returning from the palace briefing had halted by a burbling fountain to light their pipes.

The trio halted. Steve and Rogan traded stares. Then they looked at Cora. She shook her head, lips pursed. She was silently telling them there was no alternative, that this was still the only way. The eyes of the two men locked again momentarily. Each was aware just what this stroke of bad luck could mean. The uproar of a fight here in the stillness of the night would surely bring an avalanche of disaster down on their heads.

Yet they didn't hesitate.

In an instant they were leaping soundlessly from the arcade, brandishing halberd and rapier to attack with the ferocity of desperation.

There was a sharp cry of mortal agony followed by the clatter of falling weapons as the handsome captains collapsed bloodily against the well housing, dying with their swords unbloodied, never knowing who or what had killed them. Without a moment's delay the trio traversed the open width of the circular placita, expecting the alarm to sound at any moment and armed men to appear.

Yet fate decreed they should gain the welcoming shadows of a stone-walled alleyway in safety, there to be led swiftly onwards by the girl, below carved stone windows and niches containing wooden figures of both ancient gods and Christian saints, until eventually reaching the creek.

Panting heavily and perspiring hard, they gazed back. They saw the reflection of bobbing lanternlight against the walls of the placita, heard the rising sound of voices.

They didn't have much time.

They had crossed the river and were safely into the trees on the slopes before the cry went up. The bodies had been discovered. Soon lights appeared in window casements and flaming torches were to be seen bobbing along the streets as the city came fully awake.

The escapers were making good time towards the south-west corner, slogging up the steep slopes lying to the east of the cliff, invisible to any midnight watcher from above, yet anything but safe. For by this time the tunnel sentries would be on full alert, destroying any prospects the runners might have had of taking them by surprise. Yet they continued the climb with desperate haste. There was no alternative.

Abruptly Walker dropped flat and signalled the others to follow suit as they gained the ridge over which he had fled during the murderous battle between Damon's party and the defenders. Working their way upslope on their elbows, they were soon peering directly between the outcroppings upon the dark tunnel mouth and, directly above and to their left, the woods and the barricades. Walker groaned inwardly.

Where he'd estimated there to have been perhaps ten sentries posted before, there were now obviously twice that number to be seen both moving about and occupying defensive positions behind the heavy timber barricades set amongst the trees. Men with weapons were gesticulating towards the city below as they moved to and fro through dappling moonlight, armoured breastplates and helmets gleaming gold.

'No way out,' he groaned, sweat dripping off his jaw. 'But it's not too late for you, Cora. I want you to get back to the cliff and stay put. Lie about doping the guards, throw yourself on their mercy, do anything but don't stay here, honey. We've got no choice but to make a last fight of it, but it's one we're going to lose.'

Tears filled her eyes.

'I'm not leaving you again, Steve. They'll kill me

anyway, and if I have to die I'd rather die with you.'

'Judas, will you spare a man the hearts and flowers!' Rogan almost snarled. Then, 'We can't just lie doggo and wait till they find us and slit our throats, Walker. We could hide for a spell, this is a sizable basin, and we're a pair of middling tough geezers—'

His words cut off abruptly as a sudden crash of warlike sound rumbled off to the east, a booming bellow of a gunshot that washed down over the city below and came flowing up over the cliffs and ramparts and ridges to the south-west sector, seeming to suck up all other sounds in its wake until it seemed the whole basin resounded with but one noise, the harsh and ugly report of a high-powered rifle.

It was quiet for several moments before the weapon sounded again, this time loosing three successive blasts that echoed and re-echoed until all Quivira Basin seemed to tremble from end to end.

Three astonished fugitives traded uncomprehending stares. Coronado's People didn't have guns. Moments later their attention was diverted by an eruption of sudden action ahead and below as upwards of a dozen warriors came bursting from behind the barricades both mounted and afoot to go fleeing in panic away beneath the ridge along the rim of the cliff, making for the trail leading down to the city where the great brass bells in the *campanario* were now tolling the incessant alarm.

Rogan's fingers dug into Steve's upper arm.

'Don't ask me who it is, Walker, but I sure know what. It's our chance, man. Lookit these clowns below us. They're falling over one another wondering what in the Sam Hill is happening – sitting ducks.' He dropped his hand and was tucking one leg up under him, ready to rise. 'Coming? Come on. It's too late in the day to bust up a winning combination.'

'No, Steve,' cried Cora, sensing him weakening. 'It's still far too many against you.'

She was right. Walker knew it. Way too many. Even though reduced by at least half to what it had been bare minutes before, the enemy's depleted strength was still not anything to be taken lightly. Yet it remained the only faint sliver of a chance they had or were likely to be given.

A chance was still a chance.

Wordlessly he and a grim-faced Rogan were on their feet and ready to go careering downslope into the trees – that big rifle still snarling away a mile east – when an apparition erupted from the tunnel at breakneck speed.

Leastwise an apparition was what it resembled in the moon shadows as horse and crouching grey rider came storming up the slope at a racing gallop, the rider's hat tugged low, his sixgun spurting big orange gunblasts towards the barricades where men were howling in shock and rage.

Moments later the deadly thrum of bowstrings sounded and the watchers stared open-mouthed as the horseman, now clearly identifiable as a Comanchero, slipped down the far side of his running horse with one boot hooked over the cantle, Comanche style, in a desperate attempt to avoid the deadly hail.

The Comanchero gunman reached the approximate spot where Cora Lee had plunged over that night, before his horse went down on its nose, flinging the rider twenty feet. Instantly wild howls of triumph erupted from the defenders' ranks and a tall man with a yellow plume in his helmet led the rush down, screaming for blood.

How were the onlookers supposed to know this bloody play was just a preliminary, the opening gambit of a major assault? They weren't. But they were realizing it mere moments later when a swarm of howling horsemen exploded from the tunnel mouth to catch the soldiers exposed on the slope in front of them, brandishing halberds, bows and rapiers against their flaming guns.

Damon, for it was immediately seen to be him riding point with a bucking Colt in either hand, led his Comanchero squad clear through the soldiers like a sword slicing through soft cheese.

The attackers' battle plan – and it was immediately recognized as such by Rogan and Walker – was timed to the split second and was instantly and murderously successful. With their strength already halved by defections, and having quit their barricades for open ground, the brave defenders with ancient weaponry were no match for professional killers bristling with gun power and spurred on by the heady lure of yellow gold.

It couldn't last and didn't. After mere minutes of the madness of gunplay, agonized screams, gushing blood and storming hoofbeats it was over with but two of the Quivirans surviving to go racing on towards the city trail, leaving the chaos of defeat behind.

'By God and by glory!' Rogan exulted, finding his voice as he rammed a fist into the sky. 'Damon weren't kilt at all. That hardhead's just been playin' possum while he drummed up some backing to come back after getting his greedy eyes on all that gold. Can you beat that man, Walker? Ain't he something! OK, so what are we waiting for? Get square and get rich is the name of this game. Let's hustle on down there before they—'

He broke off abruptly. A stony-faced Walker had his dagger pressed into Rogan's throat.

'What the hell. . . ?'

'I'm not joining up with any butchering Comancheros here or anyplace, Rogan, not for any reason, and neither are you.' He jerked his head. 'Come on, there's nothing keeping us here now. Let's hightail.'

'You're loco!'

'We're going.'

'The hell we are!'

Rogan's halberd shoved backwards and pain seared Walker's leg. He thrust back and Rogan lurched backwards to fall and then roll swiftly from sight down the far side of the steep ridge with a howl of agony. Instantly Walker seized Cora Lee by the arm and they ran, ducking and weaving as sixgun fire erupted again behind. A bowstring thrummed and Walker glimpsed a dying Spanish soldier clutching a bow, searching for another arrow to loose at Rogan.

But Rogan vanished and so did they.

They left behind a dying bowman with nothing to occupy his last minutes but to gaze vacantly at the dimming spectacle of a huge and murderous battle surging below around the walls of the royal palace.

CHAPTER 10

WALKING DEATH

The medico applied the finishing touches to the fresh strapping he'd placed on the leg, then leaned back in his chair to squint up at his patient while he dressed.

'Coming along real good, Steve, for a gash that size, that is. Fifteen stitches! That's some stab wound, I tell you.' A momentary pause. 'And from real close, too. Right?'

Walker looked the man straight in the eye.

'Right.'

'You're a lucky man. Hell, you're both real lucky, you and Cora Lee.' He shook his head. 'Those consarned Comancheros, eh. . . ?'

'Yeah . . . those pesky Comancheros, Doc.'

That was their story, Steve Walker's and Cora Lee's. They'd told the town they'd fallen foul of Comancheros up north and had paid a heavy price.

Sulphurville had always believed Cora Lee had

died at the hands of the same 'Comancheros' who had slain Stan Chip, Walker's then partner. Walker was responsible for that lie. Upon his return to the town, believing his girl had been killed by the Quivira warriors, he'd seen no point in revealing the true story of Cora Lee's supposed death.

Neither the town nor the authorities could have done anything about it had he revealed the true story, so what was to be gained? Nothing, as he saw it.

Of course, upon his return this journey with Cora Lee at his side, he'd had to explain what had befallen the party he'd set out with. He gave them the same story, told them that, regrettably, the same wolf-pack of Comancheros had subsequently attacked himself and the Murphys in a savage gundown which also involved Joe Rogan the Sulphurville hard man, along with a group from Berbix led by the well known and 'respected' Chandler Damon, all now regrettably deceased.

The survivors' story.

Of course Steve was only too well aware that this version of things could be exposed as the lie it was at virtually any moment, should other possible survivors of the battle at the basin make it back to town. This seemed entirely possible considering the murderous confusion they'd left behind on staging their desperate break for freedom that night. Nonetheless, this would remain his story until events forced him to change it, and Cora Lee was in full agreement.

The night of the escape he had sought to illustrate to Rogan just how great a toll in human life and misery the lure of Coronado's gold had already exacted. That reinforced his determination to keep their discovery of Quivira secret, even though unaware of just how greatly that tally was to be extended before that terrible night was through. With visions of chaos still vivid in his mind there was no way he would resile from the deception he was deliberately invoking here.

In his mind's eye he could envisage the inevitable result were the true tale of the Coronadans ever to become public. How easy it was to picture overloaded wagon trains and all the hopefuls, the greedy, the gold-crazy and the downright venal or just plain crazies on horseback streaming across the badlands, raising great columns of dust into the skies as they stampeded headlong for Quivira, El Dorado or Coronado's Secret Outpost – whatever name it might be then known by, the effect would still be the same.

The great raw beauty of this magnificent frontier destroyed for ever. And more graves, always the graves.

'How much do I owe you, Doc?'

'A dollar will cover it. And make sure Cora Lee comes by for another checkout tomorrow. She's got some way to go to completely recover from her ordeal, you know.'

'You can bet I'll look after her.'

'Hmm, so I hear,' the medico said, trailing him to the door of his rooms. 'Is it true you two are making plans?'

Steve couldn't help but beam proudly.

'True enough. You're invited, of course. Matter of fact the whole town's invited to the wedding. And they'll all turn up . . . we hope.'

'You hope? Sounds like it'll be the event of the year. Who wouldn't show?'

That was not a question Steve was prepared to answer. There was no saying how Sulphurville might react should the true story of Quivira ever leak out. Quite likely if the existence of the city of gold become public knowledge, the towners would assume Steve Walker was attempting to keep it secret in order that he might exploit it. And nobody understood better than he just how ugly everyday people could turn when denied a chance of becoming rich.

He'd play those cards if and when they were dealt.

It still felt strange to walk down the street of a quiet town seeing unremarkable citizens going about their everyday business. The fantastic world he'd encountered in the Twisted Hills was still vivid in his mind, and it was as though time itself had been jolted loose in its orbit for a spell, leaving plains scout Steve Walker wondering at times which was real, today's Sulphurville or the city of the Conquistadores.

But then the storekeeper called a greeting as he passed by and the undertaker's wife nodded and smiled when they met at the butcher's, such everyday normality reminding him that the fantastic nightmare lay back in the past, that this was indeed the tranquil reality.

He paused to light up.

In the centre of the square in the shade of the chain-up tree, the saloonkeeper was again clamping a leg-iron on to rambunctious Big Olan the hellraiser, who was violently protesting against man's inhumanity to man.

Walker's smile was grim. That wild one should complain. He should see some genuine inhumanity as he had done, inhumanity fuelled by greed.

Facing northwards as he limped on towards Garvin's, he saw the heat haze still rippling over the wasteland even though this was the second week of fall. There was nothing to be seen out there, yet he imagined he could envisage the grandeur of Spanish Mountain, all calm and serene as it had been throughout the ages, brooding down upon . . . what?

What would be left of Quivira now?

He shook his head at the unwelcome thought and continued on to the watering-hole, where there were more drinkers sprawled on the porch than inside.

It was shady, cool and companionable in front of Garvin's saloon, and he relished just this kind of amiable masculine sociability. From the propped-open doors came the odour of cool beer, the voices of a bunch of seven-up players arguing gambling ethics, the soft chink of glassware.

'I'll get you one, Steve!' a friend's familiar voice called. He nodded and went to his horse which he'd left tied up in the shade. He fed the animal sugar-cubes and stroked its muzzle, wondering if anyone guessed that this was a Comanchero mustang he'd caught on the desolate plains to carry himself and Cora Lee all the long way home.

He sat with his beer and allowed the conversation to flow around him. He was still the focal point of Sulphurville's fascinated attention despite the fact that he did everything in his power to discourage it.

He wanted his latest adventure shelved and forgotten just as quickly as possible, yet he could easily understand how people might be intensely interested in something that had snuffed out so many lives.

They spoke about Damon in puzzlement, and were particularly focused on Rogan, as though finding it hard to believe that any trailsman as tough as he could really be gone.

Steve just grunted and sipped his beer, his injured leg thrust out before him, healing slowly in mind and body.

Sulphurville drowsed in the afternoon heat, today as always a peaceful village of false-fronted unpainted frame-buildings, hitch racks, the odd meandering hound – a peaceful plains town with no ambition ever to be anything more.

His appreciative eye played over the wide and dusty streets, the warped-board sidewalks, the bow-legged stride of a cowboy making his way from hotel to barn. And the six or seven contented citizens draped ungracefully in tilted chairs on either side sharing all this bucolic peace with him.

It was the realtor who dropped the front legs of his chair to the porchboards first, squinting as he shaded his eyes to stare northward.

'What's that agin' the sky out yonder? Buzzards?'

Everyone showed interest but none more so than Walker. He got up, moved to the end of the porch and narrowed his eyes. The tiny black specks against the washed-out blue of the sky far off were unmistakably buzzards.

He turned his head sharply to look at the others,

was relieved to note that nobody appeared all that excited. Could be anything dead out there, they would be thinking. Coyote, wolf, polecat. Anything. But the very uncertainty encompassed by that 'anything' was disturbing for Walker, who casually drained his glass before stepping out into the heat to limp for his horse.

'Where you goin', Steve?' someone called.

'Just moseying out there to take a look-see. Time I got a little saddle time in.'

'I'll get my hoss and come with you.'

'Don't bother, Jimmy.' He forced a grin as he settled into his saddle and jabbed a thumb at the sky. 'Trail scout weather . . . too hot for tenderfeet, don't you know.'

To his relief the drinker settled back in his chair with a lazy grin of relief. He left town at the walk, aware of a strange tingling of his nerve ends as the horse carried him past the town boundary marker and plodded towards the line of low hills that blotted the plains out of sight from the town.

It wasn't until he topped out the grassy swells some time later that he reached into his saddle-bags and produced his binoculars.

His nerve net tightened when he adjusted the screws to bring into clear sight the barely moving figure of a man on the trail directly underneath maybe a dozen of the devil birds cruising on outstretched pinions.

A man afoot coming in off the plains on a such a day. What else could this indicate but some kind of accident or disaster?

Walker glanced back over his shoulder. Nobody was following him. He gigged the Comanchero horse into a shuffling walk-trot and wondered if this might prove to be the end of his lazy days of peace and quiet. A fascinating story was just waiting to be spilled across the Kree Badlands, he brooded, and maybe, just maybe it was simply too big and momentous a series of events to remain buried.

Until the chain of events culminating in Damon leading his Comanchero henchmen into the crater on a rolling tide of gunfire, he'd been the only Outsider aware of the secret city. Then suddenly too many knew, and it would make no difference if one or a dozen survived to tell the tale, the word of Quivira's gold would be out.

But maybe he was jumping the gun. Sulphurville lay one hell of a distance from the Twisted Hills. Could be anybody.

The buzzards began flapping away with angry cries as he closed in on the figure which now lay sprawled motionless face down upon the hard-baked trail.

Steve grimaced when he glimpsed what was visible of the face. One entire side of the head and face was coated in matted blood and ripped flesh. There was an empty socket where an eye had been, raking claw marks deeply scarred half the face and ripped one bare shoulder.

This poor wretch looked as if the devil birds had been at him already!

Then he recognized what was left of a tattered black Mexican serape trimmed with gold, and felt his mouth go dry. The man was in shocking condition, emaciated, bearded, heat-blackened and torn like someone who'd emerged from the gates of hell. His hands were bloodied. The knees of his Levis were worn out and his knees were black with blood, as though he'd been crawling for miles across lacerating grit and thorny grasses. His big head hung down and he seemed to have lapsed back into unconsciousness at that moment. He was certain it was a stranger, and yet surely there was something about the breadth of shoulder and the colour of the hair that rang a faint bell?

A shadow fell across the trail and an angry screech pierced at the singing silence. Walker's .45 jumped into his fist and he triggered seemingly without aiming. But the bullet found its target and the yellow-necked buzzard exploded in a crimson smear, coarse black feathers fluttering slowly down across the trail, one actually touching the 'dead' man's head before touching ground.

The man flinched.

Walker stared disbelievingly. He would have bet money the man was already dead.

He moved the horse forward at a slow walk until its shadow fell across the man. He halted. For a moment all was still, nothing to be heard but the high-flying buzzards giving vent to their anger as they continued to circle in impatient ugliness against the sky.

The whole figure stirred and Walker grimaced as he watched in a kind of horrified fascination while that ravaged head lifted with torturous slowness until he could see the one good eye, blue and baleful, fixed upon him in an expression of scarcely human hatred.

'W-Walker!'

It was Rogan!

Steve didn't respond, made no move to step down. It was like living a nightmare. Of course he'd realized there could have been survivors, yet somehow hadn't expected Rogan to be one. It hit him brutally hard now, that he'd been guilty of wishful thinking – nothing to do with logical reasoning.

Why shouldn't the man with the iron body and the will to match be the one to survive?

Or had he survived?

The answer had to be a maybe. Although the horrific figure was drawing itself on one arm with an agonized determination that was painful to watch, the watcher who'd seen so much of death knew that Rogan was near death even if he might not be aware of it.

Rogan eventually reached the half-seated position he'd fought so hard for, but the effort had cost him dearly. His eye continued to blaze up at Walker like a shielded torch, but though his torn lips moved no words came out, not yet. His breath made a tearing sound and he shook like a man with the ague.

It was hideous. But when Walker searched himself for a touch of compassion, the locker was empty. He wasn't forgetting anything Rogan had done, how his last action had been an attempt to kill him.

Silent shadows flickered around them. The predators could smell death also. Tough Rogan was a sun-scorched, bullet-holed strip of dried rawhide, but suddenly his voice was working, faint, lacerated but audible.

'All gone, Walker, all butchered because of you . . . Damon, the Comanchero scum, all of them. You . . . you took me out of the fight when I could've made all the difference. When them Mexes counter-attacked at the palace and Damon went down, that was when they needed my class of gun to turn the tide our way again. But you sliced me, you yellow bastard, and . . . and I just had to sit and watch as they cut off Damon's head with their goddamned swords and then went after what was left of the Comancheros like they were rat-hunting! I could've saved the day, damn you! I always was the best gun on the face of these plains . . . the best man!'

He shuddered and tried to get up, but couldn't make it. His face was was something from a nightmare.

'Mexes cut me up plenty but I took the gun from a dead Comanchero and blew the bastards away. . . . Horse carried me half-way home and dropped dead. . . . I passed out for mebbe a day and the buzzards worked me over good, thinking I was a goner. But I fooled them just like I fooled you. I knew I'd make it back. Had to on account of I knew how bad you wanted me to croak so . . . so you could keep everything secret. Walked and crawled and fought off the buzzards for days, weeks, I dunno. But now Rogan's here to tell every mother's son where that gold is at . . . so wouldn't that gripe your everlasting soul, you holier-than-thou son of a bitch!'

He now shook violently like a man with the ague. The shadow of a buzzard passed across him and Rogan half-shrieked, beating frantically at the air with his right hand, the left still tucked beneath him.

For a moment it seemed he would come apart, haunted by the terror these carrion-eaters had always stirred in him. But he recovered; how, a grey-faced Walker would never know.

'And . . . and now you know you've lost out,' he continued, barely audible now, spittle running down his bearded jaw. 'That everything you done was all for nothing, I'm gonna settle with you the only way that counts. . . .'

Walker hadn't realized he'd got a gun. Both holsters were empty. But the .45 that he snaked out from a fold in his ragged serape was big, blue and frighteningly real, and he was lifting it with a determination horrifying to witness.

Walker's hand dropped on his gun handle but he did not draw. He couldn't kill a dead man even if a living corpse should kill him. That was asking one thing too many of this plainsman who'd already done and seen enough killing to last him for ever.

He was a man locked in a fatalistic trance as he simply sat his saddle and watched that gun barrel inch up towards firing level, hearing the harsh rasp of breath, the flutter of dry wings overhead. In his mind he was saying goodbye to it all, to Cora, to the great plains, to the dreams he'd revived on his journey back from hell.

Adios.

Couldn't kill again, not even to save himself.

So be it.

The gun was at firing-level. In Rogan's ruined face his one eye blazed with manic triumph as he thumbed the big gnurled hammer back with enormous effort. That fierce eye wasn't blinking. Slowly Walker realized it couldn't blink. He was staring into the eye of a dead man in a silence as deep as the grave.

The .45 thudded to the earth and the death-rattle sounded. Only then did Steve Walker haul out his sixgun and begin shooting to drive the buzzards away.

The wedding took place mid-winter and it seemed almost everybody in the badlands showed up for what turned out to be the social highlight of the year, maybe even the decade.

The happy couple honeymooned in Amarillo, and when they returned a month later there was still no news of recent strange and violent events from the north and the Twisted Hills.

Steve quietly went back to guiding folks wherever they wanted to go. He took a party of geologists out to the San Morelos fault to study ancient rocks, escorted a wagon train bound for New Mexico clear across the plainslands accompanied by a dozen armed outriders against possible attack from Comancheros. There were long jobs and short ones but none into the north until mid-spring when a group representing the Bloomfield Stage Company hired him to escort them out to Gun City, a prospective destination for the line.

The journey out proved incident-free. There were no Comanchero sightings, and indeed plains dwellers were beginning to note just how few and far between sightings of the grey scum had become in recent months.

Working his way back alone from Gun City, Walker made no conscious decision to swing south-east. But two days out on the return trail saw him emerge from the grey sameness of the plains to push his big black horse steadily towards the tortured outlines of the Twisted Hills at the base of Spanish Mountain.

It was an eerie experience, making his way afoot through the tunnel's gloom with the pearly light of next day's dawn visible ahead. He was infinitely wary upon reaching the crater rim, where he removed his hat and peered out cautiously towards the barricades.

They were overgrown with ivy and wrapped in silence.

He waited several minutes listening to the unnatural quiet before venturing out into the sunlight to make his way warily towards the rim of the cliff over which Cora Lee had vanished that terrible night.

He stopped and looked down to see nothing but silent buildings and overgrown gardens, with saplings and brush now intruding into streets, courtyards and even the houses. With his field glasses he could see bullet-peppered walls and the blackened scars where fires had ravaged the eastern end of the palace. The mine buildings had been completely demolished, were now just a mass of rubble with little about the ruins to suggest the purpose they had once served.

You could hear the quiet.

Closer inspection revealed nothing beyond the fact that everything of value or use was gone. No clues remained as to where or when the Coronadans, the Indians and their slaves had gone, or for what reason.

Maybe they'd all died in the battle he mused, as he made his return climb. Yet based on what he'd seen, backed up by Rogan's story, he very much doubted that. It seemed far more likely to him, pausing on the cliff top for one final look, that the People had simply picked up and left once they realized their long-held secret was out.

Perhaps they had set out for the homeland of Mexico of their fathers, he speculated.

Then again, being the proud and independent breed they were, he thought it likely, even probable, that they'd gone off in search of some new and even more remote home where, as they had done here, they might find the freedom to continue living the kind of life they'd followed so long as the true people of Quivira.

They were gone and he wished them well. Wherever they were, they no longer posed any kind of threat to these badlands, which he now sensed might be on the threshold of a new and more peaceful era. He believed now that Coronado's heirs had vanished for ever to become, in the fullness of time, just another fascinating legend of the great West that Steve Walker loved.